Charlie Underwood
Fights Back

PAUL MANSHIP

Gomer

Published in 2014 by Pont Books, an imprint of
Gomer Press, Llandysul, Ceredigion, SA44 4JL

ISBN 978 1 84851 827 8

A CIP record for this title is available from the British Library.

This book is published with the financial support of the
Welsh Books Council.

Printed and bound in Wales at
Gomer Press, Llandysul, Ceredigion

For Will, Simon, Alexander, Georgia, Holly, Lydia, Emily, Jarrod, Joshua, Sophia and 'Bump'

NEW BOY

The double-decker bus jolted forward, nearly sending me sprawling back down the stairs. Hanging on for grim life, I staggered towards my intended seat at the back.

A leg blocked my path, with a size nine shoe attached to the end of it.

This was exactly what I didn't need. Today of all days. Wasn't it bad enough that I was starting a new school today and had to catch a bus to get there?

'Hey dude,' said the voice that belonged to the shoe. 'I know you. You're one of Steve Underwood's little brothers. Which one are you?'

The leg remained where it was. I waited patiently, as if standing at a level-crossing.

'Give us a smile, then!' he said, lowering his leg and letting me through.

I found a seat at the back, as far away from the creep as possible, and gazed through the rain-blurred window. My new school, Our Lady's, was about a mile away from where I live. Mum had pulled me out of Brynfield – which was right next to my house – because I'd been bullied.

Dad was strongly against me moving. 'The boy's got to learn to stand up for himself,' he insisted. He's always telling me to fight back. But fighting back is a bit difficult when you happen to be the smallest kid in Year Six.

I let out a long sigh. New term, new school, new misery!

The creep stood up but, unfortunately, didn't get off the bus. Instead, he made his way towards me, a grin stretched right across his face.

He was in his early twenties. It looked as though he hadn't shaved for a day or two, but he was pretty clean and presentable, dressed in black cords and designer fleece. He sat in front of me and leaned his arm over the seat, nearly touching my knee. Alarm bells began to ring.

'So,' he said. 'It's Oliver or Charlie, right?'

I didn't respond.

'You don't recognize me, do you?' he laughed.

I did a quick scan of his face. He had short, curly, black hair, quite striking blue eyes and a jagged little scar on his chin. He tapped his fingers rhythmically on top of the seat.

'I used to be mates with your brother. We started a band together, called...'

'The Evil Dead.' It came to me. How could I not remember them? They sounded like five cats being strangled in a blender. They used to practise constantly in the garage, right under my bedroom.

That would have been about five years ago. The band members had been my older brother Steve, Gari

Lewis, Phil Meredith, Aaron Barnes and a maniac on drums who looked and played like Animal off the Muppets. A mad tornado of drumming sticks, sweat and shaggy, black hair!

This guy.

'You *do* remember!' said Steve's mate, smiling. 'I look a bit different now. I'm Charlie Brock. I was the drummer.'

Boy, he'd changed!

'Do *you* play anything?' he asked.

'Guitar,' I mumbled.

'Cool. What kind of stuff do you play?'

I hesitated. 'Metallica.'

'Wow. I'm impressed.'

He held out his hand and I shook it. 'You're Charlie too, aren't you? Am I right?'

I nodded.

His smile turned to a mock-frown. 'Why so glum?'

I explained that today was my first day in a new school and that I wasn't exactly jumping for joy about it. I continued gazing through the rain-freckled glass as the bus made its way through the estate.

'Had a bit of a rough time, have you?' he asked.

'You could say that.'

'Bullying?'

I didn't feel like going in to details.

'Didn't your teacher help?'

I shook my head. For some reason, Mr Williams, my old teacher, had seemed to think that it was partly my own fault that I was being picked on. I was too quiet and timid, Sir had said, a natural target.

My mum had complained, but that made things worse, so she pulled me out of the school, but not before telling Mr Williams and the head-teacher what she thought of both of them.

'Oh,' he said, 'that doesn't sound good. I remember I had a teacher once who locked me in the classroom cupboard!' He burst out laughing at the memory of it. 'Looking back, I probably deserved it – I *was* a bit of a handful, back then. I blocked up the urinals with chewing-gum once and caused a flood. I was suspended for that one. And another time, me and your brother left a cheese sandwich behind a radiator in the hall. It was there for weeks before the caretaker found it. The smell was atrocious. It was as if someone had died.'

I couldn't help grinning.

'What about your friends?' he asked. 'Surely you're going to miss them?'

I shrugged, 'Not really.' This was a lie though. I'd miss Daniel and Harri and Aston and a few of the others.

He looked genuinely shocked. 'Well, I know *I'd* be upset if I had to move away from my friends.'

I shrugged again. My so-called friends never seemed to stick up for me when I needed them. 'They're just idiots,' I said.

He shook his head. 'Sounds like everyone around you is a pain?'

'Pretty much.'

We sat in silence. I didn't appreciate the sarcasm.

Then he said, 'I remember when I was your age, my dad used to go on and on at me. He used to say, '*Look to no one but yourself, lad.*' He's from Yorkshire. He was always saying it. I just thought he was talking a load of old baloney. It took me a long time to understand what he was talking about. Maybe you're still too young to understand, kiddo.'

He was starting to get under my skin a bit. I didn't like being called 'kiddo' or being told I was too young to understand. What did he know?

I was about to say something when he stood up. 'Well, here's my stop,' he said, stretching. 'It was great talking to you, Charlie. Maybe I'll bump into you again, some time. Say hello to Steve for me. And little Oliver. Cheers.'

'Cheers,' I muttered, watching him pick up his bag, which was actually more like a briefcase. Maybe he was a college student or something.

He stopped at the top of the stairs and turned around. 'Listen,' he called out, 'I hope I didn't upset you by what I just said. I hope everything goes well for you in your new school. And, if you have any problems with your new teacher, let me know, I'll come and sort him out for you.'

I nodded. 'Thanks.'

I watched him get off. He glanced up in my direction, gave me a thumbs-up sign and headed into the newsagents, his briefcase held over his head to protect him from the rain.

One stop later, I got off. It was cold and wet and I was coatless.

The school gates loomed before me and beyond them lay a yard full of unfamiliar, loud kids. Some of them stopped and stared at me. One boy even pointed. I wanted to turn back.

With a deep breath, I shuffled through the gates and found a corner to hide in.

Ten minutes or so later, a pretty blonde lady in a dark blue suit strode out of the building and rang a heavy-looking bell. She spotted me straight away, introduced herself as the head, Miss Cashman, and asked me to come and line up with the rest of Year Six.

Reluctantly, I made my way over. I smiled back when a kid with scruffy hair smiled at me. He was nearly as short as me.

'Hiya,' he said chirpily, 'my name's Ieuan.' He pointed at the kid behind him. 'And he's Ryan.' Ryan lifted his head a centimetre or two but didn't say anything. He looked about as happy as I did.

Teachers began to arrive and led their classes off, one by one.

The Year Six teacher was nowhere to be seen.

The lady in the navy-blue suit, Miss Cashman, glanced at her watch and tutted. A man in a lime-green tracksuit chuckled as he walked past her.

'Dear, dear,' he smirked, tapping his watch. 'Not a good start, eh?'

She frowned.

Then, all heads turned as a frizzy-haired figure came sprinting through the gates, sporting black corduroy trousers and an expensive-looking fleece.

What was *he* doing here? It was the guy on the bus. Steve's friend.

Briefcase and newspaper under his arm, he arrived, breathless, at the front of the Y6 line.

'Mr Brock, I presume,' said Miss Cashman.

She *knew* him!

Yet she didn't look particularly glad to see him.

'Yes, sorry,' he said, offering his hand.

'They're all yours,' she declared, marching back inside the building. 'I'll see you later.'

'Oh,' he said, turning a red face towards the line. 'Looks like I've made a bit of a boo-boo. I'll have to do better, won't I? Anyway, Year Six, sorry I'm late. I'm Mr Brock and I'm going to be your teacher this year. I hope you're all going to be nice to me, as I'm the new boy around here.'

He caught my eye and winked. Spinning around, he headed towards the building, with us filing after him.

I looked up and noticed the sun trying to fight its way through a blanket of grey.

TARGET

This may confuse you, but what you've just read wasn't actually Chapter One. It was something called a prologue. A prologue is stuff that happens before the actual story, but it's still all sort of relevant.

The real story starts now – a month later.

*

Things had been building up all morning, so it was no real surprise when it all kicked off at lunchtime.

Along with my new friend Ieuan, I'd recently been given the job of register monitor, which meant that we had to get to school by a quarter to nine. Every morning we had to report to Mrs Scott, the school secretary, grab seven registers each, then set out on our deliveries.

Ieuan rushed on ahead, making a race of it.

I made my way through the hall, daydreaming, not really looking where I was going, when my pathway was suddenly blocked by what felt like a brick wall. The registers flew into the air like a huge deck of cards, loose papers shooting off in every direction and skidding across the shiny wooden floor.

A large boy stood there, arms folded, as if he'd just materialized out of thin air.

TJ Carver.

He must have been lurking behind some gym apparatus, waiting to spring his ambush.

'You ought to watch where you're going,' he said.

I set my glasses straight and started gathering up the debris. I didn't say anything. There was no point.

TJ wasn't supposed to be in the hall. He was supposed to be sitting outside the office, waiting for Mr Jackson to take him to class. (Mr Jackson is a teaching assistant, personally assigned to him. He's a pretty hefty guy, who used to be in the army.) But here he was, in front of me, and that was not a good feeling.

Things had started out pretty well at Our Lady's but, recently, the bullying had started again. I was beginning to wonder if I had a sign on me saying PICK ON ME.

I was never picked on when I was in the Infants. Maybe it was because *everyone* was little in the Infants. All Oompa-Loompas together.

But, as the years passed, I remained stubbornly small while, all around me, the other kids grew up like sunflowers. Maybe my mum hadn't given me enough water or something.

To make matters worse, my deteriorating eyesight meant that I had to wear glasses and my mum, for some reason, chose circular ones, which made me look goggle-eyed.

People usually have one of three reactions towards me. They either completely ignore me, almost unaware that I exist, or they think I'm the cutest thing ever and treat me like a puppy, or they see me as easy prey.

When TJ Carver first set eyes on me, he must have thought he'd died and gone to heaven. Here was a victim on a plate.

My first two weeks in Our Lady's had passed quite uneventfully. Mr Brock was a cool teacher. Maybe not as cool as he thought he was, but still pretty cool. There had been no bullying, which was a definite bonus. And I sort of made friends with Ieuan and Ryan, who are only slightly taller than I am.

When I first heard that there was going to be a new boy in our class, I was quite optimistic. Maybe he'd moved school for the same reason that I had. Maybe he'd been having a hard time too. Apparently, he'd left his previous school last November and had been out of school for ages. Maybe he and I could be friends.

On a day etched forever in my memory, our head-teacher, Miss Cashman brought TJ to the classroom door with his mum. I couldn't believe the size of him. He was nearly as tall as Mr Brock. And he was big-boned too. He looked as if he should be in Year Eight or Nine, not Year Six. What were they feeding him on, dinosaur steaks?

He didn't seem at all embarrassed or shy to be standing in front of a classroom of strangers. He even interrupted Miss Cashman as she was talking to Mr

Brock. 'What's that for?' he pointed. 'Where will I be sitting?' he asked, not once but twice. I could see that Miss was becoming irritated. This skyscraper of a kid was definitely not best-friend material.

It turned out that TJ had been excluded from his last school after going nuts and throwing chairs around the classroom. That's why he'd been off school for so long. No head-teacher wanted to take him on.

*

Anyway, back to the registers.

'Let me give you a hand with those,' smiled TJ, diving dramatically and sliding along the floor.

I knew this was too good to be true. I watched helplessly as he started shoving the wrong pieces of paper into the wrong registers, and doing it so roughly that he managed to rip one front cover.

I went to grab the registers off him but he pushed me away and marched off with them. 'Your services are no longer required, Midget,' he smirked. 'Take a break.'

All this wouldn't have been such a big deal but I had to endure a telling-off later that morning because the wrong registers had been delivered to the wrong classes, and all the paperwork was jumbled up. I didn't feel like explaining what had really happened. I knew there would be no point.

*

My day stubbornly refused to get any better.

After Guided Reading, we were put into groups, in preparation for a class debate. Today we were going to discuss the importance of music. And wouldn't you just know it, I was placed in the same group as TJ. Mr Jackson was supposed to be with him at all times, stuck to him like glue. Most of the time he appeared to be stuck to his laptop.

To be on the safe side, I decided that I wouldn't contribute at all to the discussion, even though I love music and have plenty to say about it. I've been learning to play the guitar for ages now and my tutor, Jason, keeps telling me I show a lot of promise. I've got two acoustic guitars and, recently, my mum bought me an electric guitar and an amp. I can play some really cool riffs by Green Day.

Anyway, I decided I was going to sit there and just say nothing.

Unfortunately, I'd agreed a personal target with Mr Brock at the beginning of the month. I had to speak up more, be more vocal. I knew that Sir would, at some point, be checking up on me.

I listened attentively to what others in the group had to say. TJ kept staring at me as if I was a strange, exotic creature that he'd never seen before.

I was itching to talk, even though I knew TJ would rubbish whatever I said. Why shouldn't I express my opinion, though? It's a free country, isn't it? And, anyway, saying nothing didn't seem to stop TJ staring at me and making me feel uncomfortable.

I took a deep breath and plunged into the conversation. 'I think that if, say for example, you're a bit of a loner, music can be your friend, sort of.'

Straight away, I wished I hadn't spoken.

TJ pounced. 'What are you talking about, geek? Music can't be your *friend*. It's a subject. That's like saying geography can be your friend or history or RE. What a loser!'

'I know what Charlie means,' said Emily, smiling at me.

'Well, you're the only one,' said TJ. 'He's just weird. Planet Earth calling Underwood.' He tapped the top of my skull. Neither of the two adults in the room spotted it. 'Anyway, I think music is a waste of time and musical instruments are stupid. Who wants to hear a flute or a clarinet or a violin anyway?'

'A guitar is a musical instrument,' I said.

'And?'

'Guitars are cool.'

'Let me guess, you play one, do you?'

I looked down at the desk. I'd never brought my guitar to school. Nobody knew I could play.

'Do you really think playing a guitar makes you cool, you dweeb?' said TJ. 'People are either naturally cool or they're not. You could be the greatest guitar player in the world and you still wouldn't be cool. I, on the other hand, don't play anything but I'm just naturally cool.'

Emily and Shannon giggled.

'What kind of stuff do you play, anyway? Let me guess. Twinkle Twinkle Little Star? Baa Baa Black Sheep? Really cool.'

'Metallica,' I muttered, but nobody heard me. They probably hadn't heard of Metallica anyway.

TJ seemed to notice that his prey had become totally silent. 'What's the matter with you?'

Mr Brock edged towards our group. He crouched down on his haunches, nudged my shoulder and pointed at my target, which was stuck to the desk. It said, *I will participate more in discussion.*

'I think,' I said, 'that music can make you happy.'

'Good point,' said Mr Brock. 'Anything else?'

'It's full of energy,' I added.

'Very true. Well done, Charlie.' Sir moved on.

TJ waited until Mr Brock was out of ear-shot and said sarcastically, 'Oh well done, Charlie. You're so smart. Anyway, you're wrong. Not all music makes you happy. What about that stuff we have to walk into assembly to? Mozart and Beethoven? That doesn't make me happy. And what about Adèle? She makes me want to slit my wrists.'

I could feel the anger bubbling up in my veins. TJ seemed to pick up on it and flipped me on the back of the head. Again, no grown-ups noticed.

'*TJ!*' said Shannon. Shannon is head girl.

'What??'

'Don't be a bully.'

'I'll do what I like,' he said. He looked as if he wanted to hit her too, but he knew better. Hitting Shannon would have been a big no-no.

'Music makes *me* happy,' said Emily, a huge smile on her face, 'tra la la!'

'Idiot,' muttered TJ.

'Two minutes!' shouted out Mr Brock. 'And then we'll have some feedback. Come on, you people who haven't said anything yet, don't forget your targets.'

I took a deep breath. 'I think...'

TJ mimicked me. 'I think...'

'... that music makes you a better person.'

'... that music makes you a better person.'

'I think...'

'I think...'

'... that I'm a moron.'

TJ didn't take the bait. He raised his hand to whack me again but, aware that Mr Jackson was glancing over, transformed the movement into a headscratch. When it was all clear, he narrowed his eyes at me. 'So, I'm a moron, am I? That's pretty brave talk, considering it'll be break-time in half an hour.'

'Why don't you leave him alone?' said Shannon.

'Look, he's crying,' whispered Emily.

I couldn't help it. I took my glasses off and wiped my eyes with the back of my hand.

'Whatever's the matter?' said Mr Brock, hurrying over.

'TJ's being horrible,' said Shannon.

'TJ?'

'What? Don't look at me! I didn't do anything. We were just having a discussion, that's all.'

Mr Brock rubbed his chin. He called over for help, 'Mr Jackson, could you please take TJ to work in the library until assembly.'

'Sure,' said Mr Jackson, jumping into action.

TJ went under protest, but not before up-ending a chair.

*

During assembly, TJ kept flicking tiny balls of blue paper-towel at me. Mr Jackson sat at the end of our row. It looked as if he was texting somebody.

TJ was an annoyingly good shot. Every little flick seemed to hit me somewhere on my face. It didn't hurt, but it was as irritating as heck. Tears rolled down my cheeks. Why me? Why was *I* the target? Why not Ieuan or Ryan or someone else?

One of the paper balls caught me right in the eye. I yelped.

Mr Jackson leant forward and hissed, 'What's going on?'

I wasn't going to say anything, but busybody Owen Jarrett did it for me. 'Sir, TJ keeps flicking bits of paper towel at Charlie.'

'Stop it,' hissed Mr Jackson.

That was it. No punishment. No consequence.

TJ glared at Owen. Maybe here was a new victim for him.

*

As we filed into the cloakroom, I stuck close to Mr Brock. I deliberately took a few moments getting my coat on because I could see TJ hovering just outside the door.

'Everything all right, Charlie?' Sir enquired.

'Don't feel very well,' I muttered.

Sir reached out and felt my forehead. 'Well, you haven't got a temperature. The best thing for not feeling well is fresh air. Out you go, now. There's a cup of coffee with my name on it waiting for me in the staffroom.'

He virtually pushed me out of the door. I checked to see who was on duty. Mr Jackson was out there, with Mr Gribbin and Miss Harris. It looked as if he was telling them both a joke.

I thought there might be safety in numbers, so I decided to join in a game of British Bulldogs that had just started.

Within seconds, TJ pushed his way into the game. Too busy keeping half an eye on me, he got tagged. As usual, he refused to take it and, as usual, because nobody was stupid enough to argue with him, he was allowed to carry on.

I'm a pretty fast runner but somebody skimmed me, which meant I became one of the catchers. There was no way I was going to even attempt tagging TJ so I concentrated on the other 'bulldogs', keeping TJ in my sights.

He looked as if he was waiting for an opportunity. He kept glancing over at the little huddle of teachers, scoffing biscuits and drinking mugs of coffee.

Something kicked off in another part of the playground and all the grown-ups turned towards it, which meant that they had their backs to the game.

Instantaneously and torpedo-like, TJ launched himself towards me.

I saw him coming and made an attempt to sidestep.

It all took place in a matter of seconds. No matter which way I went, TJ readjusted, like some sort of guided missile.

Somebody yelled, 'Watch out!' as TJ attempted to plough through me.

As we connected I started toppling backwards, and instinctively I grabbed hold of TJ's jacket. Gravity and TJ's forward momentum sent him sprawling over the top of me, hands heading towards the tarmac. To any onlookers, it must have looked like some sort of amazing judo throw.

I cracked the back of my head, and the world momentarily spun.

TJ got to his feet, red-faced and fuming. He glanced down at his hands. It looked as if he'd taken off the top layer of skin. He wasn't crying, of course. Nobody had ever seen him cry.

As everything came back into focus, I saw TJ looming over me. It looked as if steam was coming out of his ears. He swore at me and called me an idiot, raising his right boot, as if ready to stomp.

'Hey!' a voice called out.

A few boys intervened and managed to restrain TJ just as Mr Jackson came bounding over. 'Get back everyone,' he said, grabbing hold of him. 'Can I have some help over here, please?' he called over to the other teachers.

TJ momentarily broke free and kicked me in the arm.

Twice.

The pain shot through my body.

Sir grabbed hold of TJ again and frogmarched him off the yard.

TJ didn't go quietly. 'Don't touch me!' he yelled, kicking out and catching Mr Jackson with his heels.

He's gonna be suspended for that, I thought, breathing a sigh of relief. I could have a few TJ-free days.

It was a pretty heavy price to pay, though, with a lump on the back of my head, a dead arm and the wind knocked out of me.

And the knowledge that, like the Terminator, he'd be back.

CHAPTER TWO

STORYTIME

'Are you ready?' I asked Oliver at home later that night.

Oliver's my five-year-old brother. He and I were sitting on his bed.

I pressed my hand against the small lump on the back of my head and studied the huge bruise on my arm. It had to be about seven different shades of green, yellow and purple.

I share a bedroom with Oliver. He's pretty hyperactive. For quite a while now, it's been my job to read to him before he goes to sleep. As my mum values this service so highly, she pays me for it. It's not really a chore, though. I really enjoy it.

Every Saturday morning, I take Oliver to the library and we choose some books together. Sometimes, when Oliver gets bored with the books, I make up my own stories. I don't find it hard at all, which is strange because, in school, when it comes to *writing* stories, I can't seem to produce very much at all. But in the comfort of my own bedroom, I find I can make up stories on the spot, and have them finished in fifteen minutes, beginning, middle and end. My granddad was a great storyteller. Perhaps I get it from him.

I scrunched up next to Oliver, placing some pillows

behind my head and putting on my glasses. The nightlight sent fake stars across the ceiling.

Apart from when I'm messing about with my guitar, this is my absolute favourite time of the day. I have no idea where the stories come from. It's almost as if they're just floating around up there among the stars on the ceiling and I can just lasso them and pull them down.

'What's today's story, Charlie?' Oliver asked.

I had no idea what it was yet. I had to tell it first. I knew it was going to be a sort of fairytale and that there was going to be a monster in it.

I began:

Once upon a time, a very long, long, long time ago, when there was no such thing as computers, no such thing as televisions, no such thing as schools, no such thing as EastEnders and no such thing as McDonald's Happy Meals... there lived a terrifying creature called the Whomper Whoomper Snicker Snacker.

Oliver began to sink slowly beneath the quilt.

It was called 'whomper whoomper' because, when it stomped around in its Size 124 boots, it made a whomping whoomping sound – WHOMP WHOOMP WHOMP WHOOMP! And it was called 'snicker-snacker' because its sharp claws and teeth made a snicker snacker sound as it chased after animals to try and gobble them up.

'I don't like it,' said Oliver.

'It's only a story,' I said. 'It's not real.'

The Whomper Whoomper Snicker Snacker was scarily tall. Taller than any tree, taller than any house, taller even than Mrs Lewis's left leg.

'Cor, that's tall!' said Oliver. Mrs Lewis is Oliver's teacher.

It was half-giant, half-dragon.

It wore trousers and boots and a black waistcoat. It had scruffy ginger hair and a spotty, freckly face. But its eyes were red like blood, its nostrils were like two huge caves and its teeth were pointy and sharp. It had deadly claws on the end of its hairy arms and, sticking out of the back of its trousers, was a huge, heavy snake-like tail, which swooshed around behind it.

Oliver's eyes peeped over the top of the quilt.

The Whomper Whoomper Snicker Snacker lived in the Bleak Forest just outside a little village called Bettws.

Oliver sat up. 'That's where *we* live.'

'I know.' I don't mind the interruptions. They give me time to think of the next bit in the story.

Nobody from the village dared go near the forest because, although the creature had never yet eaten a human being, who could know when it might suddenly decide to? It had already eaten deer, sheep, cows, goats, horses and even a dog.

The most important person in the village was the mayor. He had put up with this monster for a long time now and had finally decided that he'd had enough. His beautiful white horse, Eira, had just gone missing, probably gobbled up by the creature. He'd already lost three horses that year.

'Not another one,' he said. 'I am most displeased. And annoyed. And miffed. Something will have to be done.'

'I agree, my Sugar Dumpling,' said his wife.

So the mayor gathered the villagers together outside The Merry Miller inn and announced, 'I hereby offer a reward for the hero who can rid our village of this annoying and dangerous beast. My daughter here, Blodwen, will marry the fellow who can save us all.'

There were no volunteers, mostly because they were terrified of the beast, but also because Blodwen was so ugly. She was uglier than a bulldog chewing a wasp.

'That's funny,' said Oliver.

The crowd parted as a boy called Charlie stepped forward.

'That's *your* name, Charlie.'

'I know.'

The villagers burst out laughing, for Charlie wasn't exactly strong or tall or handsome.

He frowned at them. 'I'll do it, but I don't need a bride. I'm too young for that.'

'What would you like, instead?' enquired the Mayor.

He paused for thought. 'I'd like a goldfish,' he said. He'd seen one in a book once and thought it looked mighty fine. 'Make that two goldfish.'

Charlie wasn't particularly clever. He could have asked for money or a job or a house but instead he chose a pair of goldfish.

Charlie's mother and father were not too pleased that he had volunteered for such a dangerous mission. Besides the fact that they loved their only son dearly, who was going to feed the chickens and milk the cows if he was gobbled up?

They had no weapons to offer him but his father put a garden fork in his hand and his mother placed a saucepan on his head for a helmet.

His dad hugged him until he turned blue and his mother cried a river as he disappeared up the lane towards the Bleak Forest.

The people of the village cheered as he rode past them on the family donkey, Neddy.

'Will he be all right?' said Oliver, concern in his voice.

'I expect so.'

The sun perched on the horizon as Charlie reached the edge of the forest. An army of trees stood before him. They swayed in the breeze and whispered, 'Don't come in!'

Oliver sank back under the quilt.

Catching Charlie by surprise, Neddy let out a loud

'Eeeaww!', threw him off and galloped away down the lane.

Charlie picked himself up and placed the saucepan carefully back on his head. 'Come back!' he yelled, his voice bouncing off the trees. 'Stupid donkey.' He held on tightly to his garden fork. He didn't need a donkey anyway.

He was just about to step into the forest when a voice called out from behind him, 'Coooo-eeee!'

'Who is it?' asked Oliver, biting his nails.

'Wait and see,' I said.

Charlie stopped in his tracks and spun around.

An old woman, dressed in rags, scurried down the lane towards him, waving a gnarled walking stick in the air.

As she got up close, he could see that she had warts all over her nose and most of her teeth were black.

'Yuk,' said Oliver, pulling a face.

'I hope – you're not – thinking – of going in there,' the old lady wheezed.

Charlie stood proud. 'As a matter of fact, I am. I'm off to kill the Whomper Whoomper Snicker Snacker.'

She shook her head and tutted. 'Foolish boy.' Pausing and rubbing her whiskery chin, she said, 'You're going to need some help.'

With that, she took out a wooden spoon, swished it through the air and tapped him on the nose three times.

There was a crackle and a spark and the garden

31

fork his dad had given him flew right out of his hand. It sizzled on the ground and seemed to vanish.

But it hadn't disappeared. It had been transformed.

It was now a pink feather duster.

'What did you do that for?' Charlie said, bewildered.

The old woman was gone. All that was left of her was a puff of purple smoke.

'That's blinking great, that is!' said Charlie. 'Do you call that help?'

There was no answer.

He took a deep breath and stepped inside the forest.

'Don't make him go in,' said Oliver, wriggling around like a fish on a hook.

'He has to,' I said, 'he's the hero.'

It was gloomy and dark, amongst the trees. Charlie's feet crunched on the forest floor. It was probably just leaves and acorns but, for all he knew, it could have been bones. The bones of all the creatures that had been gobbled up by the Whomper Whoomper Snicker Snacker.

He was aware of little eyes watching him, little rabbity eyes, little foxy eyes, little hedgehoggy eyes. Suddenly, there was a huge thumping sound and the ground began to shake. Charlie was thrown to the floor. It felt like an earthquake.

'It's the monster!' gasped Oliver, his eyes wide.

I grinned.

The leaves on the trees trembled.

Swarms of forest creatures scooted past him.

Charlie hid behind the biggest tree he could find and pressed his back right up against the trunk.

The noise died down.

Everything went quiet.

Sssshhhhhh.

Oliver gulped.

All Charlie could hear was his own breathing and his heart pitter-pattering against his ribs. Then he heard a snickering snackering sound coming from behind the tree. The sound of teeth snapping and claws cracking.

He froze, his blood turning cold. He heard breathing that was not his own.

Mum chose that moment to pop her head into the room. 'I hope you're not scaring him.'

'He's fine,' I said. 'Aren't you, Ollie?'

Oliver nodded slowly, his face as white as a ghost.

The tree behind Charlie started to jiggle about. With an enormous ripping, tearing sound, it was wrenched out of the ground and launched into the sky. A dead bird landed at Charlie's feet.

He kept perfectly still, but he knew something was right behind him. He could feel warm breath on the back of his head with a foul odour, like rotten meat.

A deep, rumbling voice groaned, 'Who dares enter the Bleak Forest?'

Oliver had now disappeared beneath his quilt.

Slowly and cautiously, Charlie turned around and came face-to-face with a head the size of a shed. The eyes were red like fire. The nostrils were big enough to swallow him up. The teeth were like daggers.

The creature smiled and said, 'What's for dinner today then, chum?'

Charlie spun around, his saucepan helmet toppling to the ground, and sprinted off as fast as he could.

'As fast as Usain Bolt?' said Oliver.

'Faster.'

'Wow.'

But, just when he thought he might make it out of the forest, his feet left the ground and he rose up towards the clouds. His feet kept right on moving. It was as if he was riding an invisible bicycle.

'Is he flying?' asked Oliver.

'No, just listen.'

The Whomper Whoomper Snicker Snacker had swept him up in its claws. Charlie was now about ten metres off the ground, face to face with the creature.

'Who are you, boy?' demanded the red-eyed beast.

'Ch-Ch-Ch-Charlie.'

'And why are you here, in my forest?'

'Th-th-the mayor sent me.'

'Did he now? Why?'

'To-to-to get rid of you?' he said nervously.

The creature roared so hard the clouds shook. 'You are either very brave or very stupid.' It stared in bemusement at the pink feather duster.

'This is my secret weapon,' explained Charlie.

'Secret?'

'Yes,' said Charlie. 'Why don't you take a better look?'

The monster pulled Charlie closer to him and, as it did so, Charlie shoved the feather duster right up its left nostril.

Its head jolted back in surprise, its eyes began to water and then it sneezed.

And sneezed again.

And again.

The monster had never sneezed before and had no idea what sneezes were. They sounded like little explosions.

At once, it began to panic, staggering from side to side and bumping into trees, all the while continually sneezing and sneezing again. And then it tripped and flipped, still hanging on to Charlie. It came down with an enormous THWOMP, cracking the back of its head on a boulder. It groaned once, then passed out.

Charlie crawled free and gawped in amazement as a white mist slithered from out of the ground and crawled all over the Whomper Whoomper Snicker Snacker.

The creature began to shrink before Charlie's eyes. Its tail fell off and shrivelled away to nothing, its claws turned into hands and its face became completely human.

It was no longer a monster. It was a young boy,

about the same age as Charlie, but much taller and with ginger hair and freckles. Charlie wasn't taking any chances. He rolled the boy over onto his belly, tied his hands together with vine and waited for him to wake up.

After making sure that he was harmless, Charlie untied him and led him back to the village, where a long-lost uncle recognized him.

'Is that the end of the story?' asked Oliver.

'Nearly.'

Charlie was hailed as a hero in the village. The mayor gave him his two goldfish. He called them Topsy and Turvy. They soon had babies of their own and their babies had babies and Charlie was able to set up his own business, selling goldfish. Oh, and he became the richest man in Bettws. The End.

'Did you like that?' I asked Oliver.

'I did, but...'

'But what?'

'I think the monster should have died. He should have been blown up. KABOOM!!'

I laughed.

Mum came in to put some clothes away. 'You really should write them down, Charlie.'

'I didn't know you were listening.'

'Well, I was.'

That was when I decided that maybe I *would* start writing my stories down. I already had about twenty or so in my head. Maybe I could get them published one day, who knows? I've always had a good imagination. Sometimes I pretend I'm a knight or a pirate or a superhero or a soldier or a gunslinger – the kind of character who nobody would want to mess with.

Unfortunately for me, I'm not able to spend all day inside my own head.

CHAPTER THREE

MAKING MUSIC

Nine-thirty. Thursday morning.

A pile of encyclopedias sat in front of me, along with a tricky set of questions. I shook my head in frustration. I was having major trouble finding out which was the third longest river in the world.

I glanced at the clock. Sir had already sent the registers back to the office. TJ was due back in school today, but there was no sign of him as yet. I began to relax.

Moments later, a huge row erupted just beyond the classroom door. At first, I thought that it was Miss Cashman telling someone off, but then the door flew open and TJ came staggering in. A desk prevented him from flying right across the length of the room.

'Get in there and stop arguing!' snarled the woman who stood in the doorway, her arms folded. TJ's mum.

'I don't wanna go,' he said, trying to barge past her.

'I don't care what you want,' she yelled. 'You ain't staying home with me.'

'I wanna go fishing with Jordan.'

'Well, you ain't going. Not after last night. Get in there.'

With that, she pushed him sprawling onto the carpet. He lay there like a wounded animal.

Mr Jackson helped him up and ushered him towards the computer.

'Mrs Carver,' protested Mr Brock, leading her outside, 'could I have a word?

We could all hear some of the very vocal conversation that followed. TJ's mum's voice went from loud to LOUD to **LOUD**.

When Mr Brock came back in, Mr Jackson had set up a computer game for TJ. Reluctantly, he put on some headphones and began to play. Unfortunately for me, he happened to catch me staring at him. It didn't matter that the whole class was staring at him. I was the one he spotted.

'What do you think you're looking at, Midget?' he snarled.

I looked away instantly. But it was too late.

TJ picked up a rubber and threw it. It skimmed the top of my head and bounced off the window.

Mr Brock made a sign for Mr Jackson to take TJ somewhere else, which he did, after a struggle.

Sir took a deep breath. 'Right then,' he said to the rest of us, 'let's keep calm and carry on, shall we? Are you okay, Charlie?'

I felt the top of my head and nodded, a bit stunned by the whole episode.

*

That afternoon, when Ieuan and I arrived back in class after handing out the registers, we found that all the desks and chairs in the classroom had been pushed towards the edges of the room and that all our classmates were sitting on the carpet in a big circle, each person with a musical instrument in front of them.

'Find a space, you two,' Mr Brock told us.

There were only two spaces left. On either side of TJ. Understandably, we were pretty slow to occupy them.

All the best instruments were gone. I was left with a wooden block.

'Right,' Sir began, 'let's make a start, shall we? Today we're going to focus on rhythm. As you know, I used to be a drummer. Still am. Once a drummer, always a drummer.' He started tapping his desk. 'Hands up if you think *you've* got rhythm.'

All the girls raised their hands in the air and about half the boys.

Sir stopped tapping and nodded. 'Well, we'll soon find out, won't we?'

He grabbed a chair and sat himself in the middle of the circle. He started by clapping out some rhythm patterns, which we had to clap back at him. The rhythms became more and more complicated.

Generally it sounded pretty good, but it soon became obvious that TJ had no sense of rhythm whatsoever. Sir clapped 'tah-tati-*tah*-tah', which any four-year-old could copy – but TJ's effort sounded more like 'tati-tati-tati-tati-tati-tat... i...' In fact, *every* rhythm that Sir clapped out, TJ's reply sounded like 'tati-tati-tati-tati-tati-tati...' Like an over-wound clockwork monkey.

TJ leaned across, gave me a shove and smiled as if he was having the best fun ever.

Sir's rhythm patterns became more and more complicated, but TJ seemed to be stuck in some sort of loop. A 'tati-tati-tati-tati' loop. It was starting to get to me but eventually, thankfully, the clapping game came to an end.

'Right,' said Sir, 'you may now pick up your chosen instruments.' *Chosen? That* was a joke. The block had chosen *me*.

Within seconds, there was pandemonium. Twenty-four of us, all improvising at the same time.

'*Put* them back down again,' yelled Sir. 'I didn't say *play* them, did I? I said pick them *up*.'

'Yeah, plonker,' said TJ, flicking me on the arm with his tambourine.

'That's a warning, TJ,' said Sir. 'Keep hands, feet and objects to yourself.' (That's one of our six school rules. The six rules that TJ doesn't seem to have to abide by.)

'Right,' Sir said, 'we're now going to work in groups. I think four groups should be enough. Each group will have one person whose job it is to keep a nice, steady *one*-two-three-four beat using the wooden block.'

That would be me, then.

'I'd like the other people in each group to use their instruments, one by one, to devise repeated patterns to play over the top of the steady beat. A word of warning, though. You can't just play *any* old thing, otherwise it'll sound like bedlam. You *have* to keep that steady beat in the back of your mind, like a ticking clock, and fit your pattern around it. *Tick* tock tock tock, *tick* tock tock tock...'

Each group picked up their instruments and arranged themselves in a little circle. I sat opposite TJ. As soon as Sir's back was turned, he snatched Ryan's bongos and threw him his tambourine.

'Right,' said Sir, taking centre stage again, 'take a minute to think about what you're going to do. You may even want to clap it all out first.'

About five headache-inducing minutes passed by. When Sir could take it no longer, he brought proceedings to a halt.

Our group was asked to perform first.

TJ grinned at me, 'Take it away, block-boy.'

I took a deep breath and started beating my wooden block steadily and rhythmically.

After eight beats, Owen, who was on my right, joined in. He had a triangle and, quite sensibly, kept it simple with *ting*, ting, ting-a-ling, *ting*, ting, ting-a-ling...

After a few more beats, we gave TJ the nod, whereupon he proceeded to pound away on the bongos like a Tasmanian devil! Thankfully, Mr Brock stopped him almost immediately. 'Aaarrrgghh! TJ, stop! Take it easy, take it easy! You've completely lost the rhythm. Ryan, swap instruments with him, please.'

TJ snatched the tambourine out of Ryan's hands, leaving him to pick up the bongos.

We started again. I hit the wooden block eight times, Owen did his triangle ting-a-linging bit and then Ryan came in with this groovy rhythm on the bongos – *binga* banga bong-bong, *binga* banga bong-bong... Sir looked quite impressed! We were starting to sound pretty darn good.

Ieuan joined in. He held this big, ribbed, shiny metal cylinder in one hand and a large fork-shaped scraper in the other. Surprisingly, he did a pretty good job of it. His pattern went something like this: *sk*uh-uh-scraaaape, *sk*uh-uh-scraaaape, *sk*uh-uh-scraaaape... e... e...

We sounded cool – it was quite funky, a bit like jazz.

And then it was TJ's turn. He started pounding on the tambourine like there was no tomorrow, completely out of rhythm and totally off-the-beat. There was absolutely no pattern to it. He was all over the place.

However, *he* was obviously under the impression that what he was playing was amazing, because his eyes were closed and he had a huge grin on his face.

He kept banging away, oblivious to everything and everyone, even after the rest of us had stopped.

Sir crawled over towards him and said 'Oy!!!' about two inches away from his left ear, causing him to drop the tambourine instantly.

I caught Mr Brock's attention and pleaded, 'Can I *please* go in someone else's group?'

Mr Brock sighed. 'Are there any volunteers willing to swap places with Charlie?' he asked.

Tumbleweed time. No takers.

'Sorry, then,' said Sir. 'You'll have to stay as you are. You can swap instruments again if you want to.'

Sir swapped TJ and Owen's instruments. TJ now had a triangle.

I picked up the wooden block for the third time and tapped out eight steady beats. TJ had to follow me this time. But he wasn't ready and missed his turn completely. He held the triangle by its leather strap, but had somehow managed to twist it so that the triangle kept spinning round and round as he tried to strike it. He clearly found this hysterically funny, but I felt like I wanted to ram TJ's head *through* the triangle.

Sir let out a deep sigh. 'I think you'd better have the wooden block, TJ.'

Grateful at last to get rid of the block, I passed it over.

TJ dumped the triangle in my lap.

There was no way he could go wrong this time.

Even an idiot could hit a wooden block with a steady rhythm.

It was not to be, though, because even though the rest of the group counted the rhythm out *for* him – **1**-2-3-4, **1**-2-3-4, **1**-2-3-4 – TJ still managed to hit the block *off* the beat every single time. It was almost as if he was doing it on purpose. He could see how annoyed we were getting and he was deliberately winding us up!

My head pounded. It felt as if someone had turned the volume right up to eleven. The wooden block no longer sounded like a wooden block. It sounded like a sledgehammer, banging against the inside of my skull.

Beat and **bang** and **bash** and **thump**...

Meanwhile, TJ cackled away like a lunatic in an asylum.

... and **hammer** and **crack** and **batter** and **thwack**...

He was laughing so hard that tears were rolling down his face.

... and **thud** and **slam** and **pound** and **boom!**

Inside my head, something snapped. I grabbed the block out of TJ's hands and threw it, full force, across the room. It sailed past his head and hit the classroom door with a horrendous crack, then rebounded and landed with a clatter in the instrument trolley.

The class symphony came to an immediate and abrupt halt. Every member of the orchestra had been transformed into open-mouthed goldfish.

'Holy cow,' Ieuan muttered under his breath.

Mr Brock, who'd had his back to us and hadn't seen the actual launch, turned towards us with a face completely drained of colour. '*Who* threw that?' he demanded, staring straight at TJ.

'Don't look at *me*,' TJ scowled.

'It wasn't him,' Mr Jackson piped up.

Mr Brock took another guess. 'Ieuan?'

Ieuan shook his head. 'Nuh-uh.'

From the corner of my eye, I spotted Owen pointing, right at me. I'd always felt kind of sorry for Owen, but not any longer. At that moment, I wanted to separate him from his life.

Sir looked confused. 'Charlie?'

My gaze was fixed firmly on the carpet.

'Charlie?' Sir repeated.

My eyes didn't move.

'Did *you* do it?'

'Do what?'

'Do *what*?' he said, exasperated. 'Did you just throw that block at my door?'

His door? I thought.

Mr Brock persevered. 'Well, *did* you?'

'Yes,' I muttered.

Sir was visibly shocked. '*Yes?* You amaze me! Any reason why?'

'I missed.'

'*Missed*! Missed what?'

I shrugged. It was obvious, wasn't it?

Mr Brock looked lost for words. 'You astonish me, Charlie. Well, I'm sorry, but I can't have people throwing missiles around my classroom. It's not safe. You could have put somebody in hospital! Ieuan, would you please take Charlie to Miss Cashman's office.'

I used Owen's shoulder to lever myself up and was out of the door before Ieuan could even stand up.

'Hey, hold up!' Ieuan called after me, but I maintained my stride.

'Hey, Charlie, what the heck's up with you?' he asked, concerned.

I wasn't in the mood for talk. My head throbbed, as if there was a whole troupe of stonemasons inside there hammering away.

He left me at the office-door, wishing me good luck.

*

Thankfully for me, I didn't come out of it too badly.

Miss Cashman was obviously concerned about my outburst – which she said was uncharacteristic – and the fact that I'd damaged school property, but she was quite sympathetic towards me and wanted to know if I was okay.

It dawned on me how stupid I'd been. I'd completely over-reacted. It wasn't as if someone had insulted my mother or thrown my PE kit down the toilet. All TJ had done was play a musical instrument very badly.

I wanted so much to tell her all about TJ, but I just couldn't. I was beginning to wonder if, in some way, I'd brought my problems on myself. If, in some weird way, I was asking for it. And what good would telling do, anyway, in the long run? It was highly unlikely that TJ would be expelled, so it would only make things worse.

'I hope this isn't the *start* of something,' said Miss Cashman. 'Do you feel that it is?'

'No, Miss,' I replied, although I couldn't exactly be sure. 'I'm just in a bad mood and having a bad day.'

'Well, we all have those, that's for sure,' she smiled. 'However, I can't have people throwing things around classrooms, damaging property and endangering other pupils. I'd like you to apologize to Mr Brock before you go home. Tomorrow, at break-time, you'll have to stay in and fill out a think-sheet. Meanwhile, I think you'd better sit outside my office for a while, until you have fully calmed down.'

I nodded.

'Do you want me to have a little word with TJ?'

'No thanks.'

What would be the point? You can't reason with a gorilla.

CHAPTER FOUR

SHARKBAIT

Mr Brock was quite forgiving towards me too.

Predictably, TJ wasn't. If I hadn't been before, I was now definitely Number One on his hit-list.

'Summer Term looks like it's going to be pretty hectic,' said Mr Brock later that afternoon, standing by the window. 'So much will be happening over the next few weeks, we won't know whether we're coming or going. On Monday, as you know, we'll be starting swimming lessons.'

My heart sank. To say I can't swim is the understatement of the year. There are rocks that can swim better than I can. My mum tried to take me for lessons when I was younger, but I didn't even make it past the first lesson. I got as far as the water's edge, then passed out, cracking my head on the side of the pool on the way down. There was blood everywhere.

I contemplated being ill for the next three weeks, but I knew Mum and Dad would never let me get away with it.

Sir explained that, during the swimming sessions, we'd be put into three groups: Sharks, Dolphins and Minnows. 'Hands up,' he said, 'if you're a confident swimmer and you can swim, say, more than ten lengths.'

Three hands went up – Seren, Stephanie, and TJ. If Sir had asked who had swum the Atlantic Ocean, no doubt TJ's hand would have been in the air.

'How far can you swim, TJ?' Sir asked, looking a bit doubtful.

'Dunno, about a mile,' TJ replied.

About fifteen of my classmates said they could swim about a length. These would be the Dolphins.

'Now, please don't be embarrassed,' said Mr Brock, 'but put your hands up if you can only swim a few strokes, or even not at all.'

How could we *not* be embarrassed? Saying you can't swim is like admitting you can't tie your own shoe-laces. About eight hands rose reluctantly into the air. TJ was already sniggering. Mr Brock told him to shush.

'I promise you,' said Sir, 'all of you, you'll thoroughly enjoy the next three weeks and if you can't swim now, I bet you'll be able to by the end. You'll all be confident in the water and you'll all be able to enjoy those holidays abroad with your families.'

I gulped.

TJ stared at me. He reached up and gripped his throat with both hands, sinking slowly to the carpet, as if he were drowning.

Sir spoke to me as the rest of the class headed off home for the weekend. 'Don't let TJ put you off,

Charlie. You'll be in a small group with Ian, the swimming instructor, and nobody will make you do anything you don't want to do, I promise.'

TJ mimed swimming past the door. He sang the theme tune from Jaws as he watched me get on my bus. As I looked down from the top-deck window, he made fish-faces at me.

*

When Monday came around, I had to use the toilet three times before breakfast.

'I don't feel well,' I groaned across the breakfast table.

'I didn't think you would,' said Mum.

'I've just remembered I haven't got a swimming costume,' I said.

She lifted an Asda carrier bag from under the table. 'I know. That's why I bought this for you on the weekend.'

I looked in the bag at the huge, brightly-coloured Bermuda shorts she'd bought for me. At least she hadn't got Speedos.

'I haven't got goggles. Sir said you need goggles.'

'I know. I bought a pair of those too. They're in the bag, along with a towel. Here's a pound for the locker.' And she handed me the coin with an extra bright smile.

'Listen, I know you're a bit nervous,' she said, 'but

learning to swim is really important. It could save your life one day. I wish I'd persevered with you when you were younger. I'm sure that, once you get today over, you'll really enjoy it.'

I shrugged, then took in a few deep breaths.

Oliver stopped eating his Coco-Pops and started singing, 'I know a song that'll get on your nerves', over and over and over...

Mum's mouth was still moving but I couldn't hear what she was saying. I felt like a human kettle.

'I know a song that'll get...'

'SHUT UP, WILL YOU!!!' I yelled, slamming my fist on the table and causing some of Oliver's cereal to take flight from the bowl. I grabbed the Asda bag and stormed out of the door.

'Charlie!' Mum called after me.

'I'll miss the bus,' I yelled.

Trudging towards the bus stop, I seriously contemplated skiving off for the day.

Swimming wasn't until the afternoon. Meanwhile, for the rest of the morning, at every opportunity, TJ kept up with the Jaws theme and fish-faces.

It was a ten-minute walk to get to the pool, through the middle of the estate. We were arranged in pairs. I found myself with Owen Jarrett. It was boiling hot outside. Mr Brock was at the front of the line in his dark blue t-shirt and tracksuit bottoms. Mr Jackson brought up the rear. He isn't allowed to wear short-sleeved shirts because of his tattoos, apparently.

TJ is one of those people who can't even do a simple thing like walk from A to B without doing something he isn't supposed to. One of the rules Sir had laid down before we left the school building was no overtaking but, within two minutes, TJ had already overtaken six pairs and, at the petrol station, our journey's halfway mark, he was right behind Owen and me. He started making 'glug glug glug' sounds.

'You're not supposed to overtake, y'know,' Owen said to him.

'Shut up, Sheriff Know-it-all Jarrett.'

We veered off the main road and followed a path alongside the Brook which, as usual, was full of rubbish.

I felt something flick the back of my neck. Some of the kids behind us giggled. I turned around as TJ reached into the bushes, pulling out a few of those long green seedy things that have Velcro-like hooks that stick to your clothes. I reached back over my shoulder. There was one already on my jumper. I brushed it off. TJ threw another one to replace it. I took my jumper off and put it into my carrier bag. The seeds wouldn't stick to my shirt.

I was so busy trying to sort myself out that I nearly collided with a pushchair.

'Watch where you're going, luv,' a disgruntled lady said.

'Yeah,' repeated TJ, 'watch where you're going. Don't you care about other people?'

I heard Mr Brock call out 'Cyclist coming!' A middle-aged man in dirty grey overalls, was heading towards us. It looked as if he was on his way to work.

'Move over, everyone!' yelled Sir.

The kids in front of us shifted over, leaving a clear pathway for the cyclist. The bike drew closer and was nearly past me when I felt a thud in my back, which caused me to sprawl towards its back wheel. My leg actually made contact with it, causing it to wobble.

The cyclist didn't stop. Instead, he glanced back over his shoulder and shouted 'Idiot!'

'Are you okay?' said Owen, helping me up. Sir was facing the wrong way and Mr Jackson was looking at something on his phone. 'I'll go and tell sir.'

'Don't bother,' I said.

'Yeah, don't,' said TJ. 'Really.'

Finally, we arrived at the high school.

Sir told us to be extra quiet as we made our way through the entrance and past the main reception. I could smell the chlorine already. A mob of high school boys came piling out of the changing rooms, making enough noise to wake the dead. At that moment, I pretty much wished that *I* was dead.

Ian, the instructor, was there to meet us, dressed in white t-shirt and black shorts and smelling strongly of Lynx. Short and muscular, he had dazzling white teeth when he smiled, like you see in the adverts.

After just being told not to run, my classmates swarmed past me into the changing rooms. Thankfully, there were individual cubicles. As I undressed, my heart pounded away like a volley of depth charges. I had to tie the cord really tight to keep my new Bart Simpson shorts up.

Reluctantly, I joined the other kids, poolside. Ian told us all to stand up straight, against the wall. Like a firing squad. I could feel the cold tiles pressing against my back.

I had taken my glasses off which, I knew, made my eyes look kind of funny. I crossed my arms in front of my chest.

TJ was wearing red Speedos. They showed off his strong and chunky physique. He glanced across at me. 'OMG,' he sneered, 'you look like a skeleton. I can see your ribs. Your knees stick out. Why are your eyes so weird?'

'Have you finished?' said Ian the instructor, sternly. 'Any more of that nonsense and you can get out.' He turned towards Mr Brock. 'Is he in my group, Sir?'

'Uh, no,' said Mr Brock, embarrassed.

TJ pulled a face.

We were quickly sorted into our three groups. Mr Brock took the Dolphins up to the middle of the pool and Mr Jackson went off with the three Sharks.

Eight nervous children stayed with Ian. I noticed water shadows dancing on the pool walls. I felt suddenly faint and would have fallen in if Ian hadn't told us to sit and dangle our feet in the water.

Thankfully, for the next fifty minutes, I was allowed to exist in a completely TJ-free zone. Occasionally, I took a furtive glance towards the deep-end to see what he was up to. He was as good as he said he was. When he swam, he cut through the water as if it wasn't even there. Like an actual shark.

I took a huge amount of persuading, but eventually lowered myself into the water. All the others in my group were already dipping their faces in, even blowing bubbles. I'd need more time.

We had running races across the pool. My legs felt like lead, but it was good fun – almost like running on the Moon – except for the moment when I slipped and nearly went under.

We were given some floats and practised our kicking techniques. I found myself relaxing and quite enjoying it. The water had been freezing at first but, the more active I was, the warmer I became.

I hadn't learned a lot by the end of the first lesson but at least I'd managed to get into the water and I was ready and willing to come back the next day. I felt a lot more confident and Ian patted me on the back in approval.

We were allowed ten minutes' free time before we had to climb out of the pool. Ian threw some large floats into the pool and some soft balls. At first I hung firmly onto the side. There was far too much noise and movement and splashing going on. But Ryan persuaded me to take a walk further down the pool and play catch. I was actually starting to have fun.

I reached for one particularly high ball, but it grazed my fingernails and shot over my head. As I turned around to retrieve it, TJ was there, holding it in his hands.

'Come and get it, scaredy-cat,' he taunted.

Even though TJ was further down the pool than I was, I could see that his chest was still above water, so I moved gingerly towards him. As he backed away slowly and kept moving back, I went with him. Before I knew it, I was on my toes and I couldn't stop my forward momentum. Some water slid into my open mouth. I panicked and fell forward into even deeper water. My feet were no longer touching the bottom. I reached out to pull myself up, but pulled myself the wrong way. I rose and sank like someone on a bucking bronco, my legs riding an invisible bike. I tried to call out, but my mouth wouldn't open.

The next thing I knew, I was being lifted under my arms and carried towards the edge of the pool, Seren and Steph on either side of me. It couldn't have been any more humiliating.

After a lot of coughing and spluttering, the lifeguard gave me a bit of a telling-off for wandering past the cut-off point. I was too distressed to try and explain what had happened.

TJ was down at the deep-end, diving for bricks. Was he completely oblivious to the fact that I had nearly drowned? Did he actually have any feelings towards other human beings? He seemed to act purely on instinct, doing whatever entertained him, made him laugh.

What made it worse was that I knew that this time I was actually partly to blame. After all, I was the one who had wandered into water which was too deep for me. I didn't *have* to go so far down the pool and I didn't *have* to go after that stupid ball.

Ian sat me down and made sure I got my breath back. My classmates seemed genuinely concerned. All except TJ, who found it all extremely amusing.

Our hour was up, so Sir ushered us towards the changing rooms. I made my way to my locker, taking the key-band from around my wrist. The locker was already open and it was empty.

I stood there, a silent island amid an ocean of noise.

I couldn't help it. I started crying, my chest heaving uncontrollably.

I felt an arm on my shoulder. It was Stephanie. 'Okay Charlie?'

'No – I'm – not,' I gulped. I know I must have sounded ridiculous.

'What's wrong now?' said Mr Brock. Did I detect a note of irritation in his voice?

'He's hidden my clothes!!' I sobbed.

'Who? TJ?'

I nodded.

Sir looked confused. 'But how could he get into your locker? You've got the key. Unless you left it open.'

Had I left it open? I couldn't remember.

Ian came up from behind us. 'Maybe he didn't lock it properly, Sir. It's got to click into place.'

I started to panic, desperately running around, searching on the floor, in the toilet, in the showers.

'What's wrong?' said Mr Jackson, his face red and sweaty.

'He's – hidden – my – clothes!' I sobbed.

Mr Jackson looked bewildered. 'He couldn't have. I've been with him the whole time.'

'I didn't do it,' TJ yelled from somewhere inside his cubicle.

'You can't keep accusing him of everything, y'know,' Mr Jackson said.

'But he did it,' I yelled, 'I *know* he did it.'

'What's wrong?' said Owen, who was already dressed, despite being still soaking wet.

'TJ's been in my locker and hidden my stuff.'

'No I haven't, you liar,' yelled a disembodied voice.

Owen scratched his head. 'But your locker is around by here next to mine. Number 72.'

I felt like an idiot. I'd been looking in Number 12. I didn't have my glasses on. 'Oh,' I said.

'I think you've got yourself in a bit of a state,' Mr Brock said. 'Try and calm down. Take a few deep breaths.'

Mr Jackson, who was leaning against a cubicle door, said, 'I think you owe TJ an apology, Charlie.'

'What?' I said, exasperated. '*He* owes *me* an apology for picking on me all the time.'

'I ain't apologizing to no-one!' TJ said, emerging from his cubicle, still wiping his hair.

All of my pent-up anger was suddenly released. I charged straight at TJ, cracking his head against the cubicle door.

TJ's eyes opened wide. He grabbed me by the neck. 'I'll kill you!' he yelled, pushing me back into the teachers.

Mr Jackson managed to release TJ's hold and manhandled him outside.

Mr Brock shook his head. 'Charlie, go and get changed. You're not helping matters. I need to speak to you when we get back to school.'

'Me?'

'Yes, you.'

*

We headed back to school along the Brook.

My eyes were red, from the chlorine and from the tears. I felt ashamed. Everyone would think I was a baby.

We were about halfway home when I heard someone near the front of the line making 'Euuuggh!' noises. There was a lot of pointing going on.

Up ahead there was a dog, down on its haunches. It was so big it looked as if it should be wearing a saddle. A Great Dane. It had its back legs spread apart, frog-like, and it was making little yelping noises, obviously in some distress.

Some stuff was pouring out of its backside. Orange-brown sludgy stuff spreading out on the ground, forming a mini-lake. The stench was beyond belief, even from this distance.

The owner of the distressed animal, a scruffy looking bloke with long greasy hair, didn't look at all embarrassed. He just tugged on the lead and pulled the dog away. There was still stuff dripping from its behind, like curry, as it moved off. The sludgy puddle it had left behind now covered half the width of the path.

In single-file, we made our way forward. As we approached the offending mess, everyone pinched their noses. Some made gagging noises.

At that moment, I would have felt a lot happier with TJ in front of me, where I could see him. There was no way that he would let an opportunity like this pass by. I took a quick glance over my shoulder.

Owen was directly in front of me. He bypassed the swampy puddle by performing a little run on tip-toes.

I hesitated. That dog must have been seriously ill. I'd never seen dog poo like it before. It had the consistency of liquid cement, unfortunately without a similar colour or smell.

I felt a nudge in the small of my back. TJ.

'Go on, Underpants! Hurry up.'

I took a step forward, but felt an even harder nudge, causing me to bend over in the middle, my face hovering right over the poo, my feet balanced momentarily on the tips of my toes.

'Sir!' Owen called, trying to help out, but Mr Brock was already striding ahead like an explorer on an expedition.

I could sense that TJ was going to go for one more push. Instinctively, and swiftly, I crouched and pulled back at the same time.

TJ must have reached out and missed because he went sprawling over the top of me. He missed the poop by the merest of millimetres, but his bag landed partially in it.

'Oh my god!!' he yelled, jumping to his feet.

Mr Brock was there in a flash. 'What happened?'

'He pushed me,' growled TJ.

Sir helped me to his feet. 'Is that true, Charlie?'

I shook my head.

'What happened, Owen?'

Owen paused for the briefest of seconds. 'TJ fell,' he said. Wisely, he didn't add 'while trying to push Charlie into the poo.'

Sir scanned the scene. 'Looks as if it was just an accident.' He held TJ's sports bag in the air. It had been contaminated. Carefully, he pulled out the towel, costume and goggles and handed them to Mr

Jackson, who'd just arrived on the scene. He pulled out a black bin-bag from his own rucksack and placed TJ's bag in it, tying a knot in the end.

'How did you get up here?' Mr Jackson said, breathless.

TJ's eyes virtually drilled into my face. 'You're dead meat.'

Mr Brock took a deep breath. 'Oy, do you want to come swimming tomorrow or not?'

'Don't care,' said TJ.

Sir gave Mr Jackson a look. 'Keep an eye on him.'

After all, I thought, that's your job. Your *only* job.

CHAPTER FIVE

BLACKHEART

I felt as if I was going to explode.

I ran into the newsagents on the way home and bought myself a notepad. Heading straight into my dad's study, I began to write. It was as if the words had been waiting there for ages, ready to burst their banks and pour from me. I kept at it for three hours, only stopping to eat.

It was pretty violent and bloodthirsty stuff, not the kind of story I could read to my five-year-old brother.

It went like this:

Of all the pirates who sailed the Seven Seas, more greatly feared than Blackbeard, Henry Morgan, Barbarossa, Calico Jack and Captain Kidd, was Carver Jones, also known as Blackheart.

He was, by far, the tallest of the pirate leaders, being at least six foot six, with wide shoulders and skinny limbs. His hair was long and black, like raven feathers, his face gaunt and haggard, almost skeletal, and his eyebrows permanently arched, framing dark eyes with no more life in them than a shark's. Sharp sideburns etched the sides of his cheeks. He wore a permanent sneer, a result of the scar that marked one side of his face.

He wore a red bandana and two large hooped earrings. His coat was long and black, and swept dramatically from side to side as he strode about. One of his sleeves was cut away at the elbow, revealing a cutlass blade where his forearm should have been. It was rumoured that he'd had an encounter with a tiger shark off the coast of Cuba, in which the shark had come out on top.

Beneath his coat, he wore two pistols across his chest but, what was perhaps most intriguing about him, was what was supposed to lie behind the pistols. Legend had it that he didn't have a living human heart. The heart that perched inside his rib cage was supposed to be black and shrivelled, with no more life in it than a fossil.

Woe betide any crew unfortunate enough to have their ship captured by Blackheart and his men. If they didn't join him, he would have them killed, in cold blood. And, if they did decide to join his crew, their souls would become his.

Young Charlie Hodge put all thought of Blackheart to one side. He was too busy performing his various duties. Captain Brock took up a lot of his time. Charlie had to mend his clothing, maintain his wig, polish his shoes, serve him at dinner, prepare his bath, help him shave and dress, run various errands and so on.

He also had to wait on the officers, polish the brass and silver, trim the wicks of the lamps, change the bedding, clear up after dinner, dust, sweep, take *messages, scramble up the rigging to trim the sails when they needed trimming, stand watch, even help out as helmsman, when the weather was fair. He was also pretty good at holding the ship on a steady course.*

Charlie was twelve years old and, for the most part, well-treated. The men considered him their mascot. The worst they did to him was tell him a few scary tales.

Able Seaman Dudley told one which he couldn't get out of his head, no matter how hard he tried. In 1788, apparently, two sailors and a cabin boy were shipwrecked and cast adrift in a small boat without provisions. To save themselves, the sailors killed the cabin boy and ate him. Actually ate him. They were convicted of murder, despite their claimed defence of necessity.

That story gave Charlie nightmares for weeks afterwards.

*

It was Sunday morning. A calm day with a slight breeze. The sun sat high in the sky, a golden doubloon resting on blue velvet.

The Royal Fortune cut smoothly through the gentle waves, led by a school of playful dolphins.

The captain had just said a few prayers and read some passages from the Bible. The crew were busy cleaning and polishing. They sang sea shanties. Charlie's favourite was 'Cheer Up My Lively Lads.' A good mood prevailed.

Charlie was up on deck, enjoying a short rest. He sipped some of his grandmother's Recipe. This was a cure-all she had invented. She knew about herbs and spices and suchlike. When she discovered that he intended to run away to sea, she gave him three bottles of it.

Two months in and he had a gnawing toothache, which is why he was taking a swig from one of the bottles. He perched next to the oldest hand on board, Billy Griddle, who was teaching him how to whittle. Billy had been telling him all about Blackheart.

'Still, there be no danger of us meeting him on this trip,' said Billy. 'He's been lying low for close on a year now. Rumour has it that his bones be resting in Davy Jones' Locker.'

Charlie stopped working and glanced heavenwards. 'That's a big gull,' he pointed.

Billy lifted his cap to shield his eyes from the sun. 'That's no gull. That be an albatross.'

'How can you tell?'

'By its size. Looks like a twelve-footer. Supposed to bring good luck.'

There was a sudden loud bang and the albatross's wings wavered.

Johnny Jarrett held a smoking musket in his hands. He was laughing like a loon.

Billy growled, ran over and knocked it from his hands. 'You'll be getting us all killed, you weed-choked barnacle.'

"Tis just a bird,' said Johnny.

'Are you blind? Can you not see it's an albatross? And killing an albatross is the worst luck of all.'

'I didn't kill it, did I?' shrugged Johnny, turning pale.

Other members of the crew had gathered around to see what all the fuss was about. Someone made the sign of the cross.

Thankfully, bad luck didn't come to pass. No storm struck them. If anything, the weather improved.

*

On the third day following the albatross incident, as Charlie stood next to the chief helmsman at the prow of The Royal Fortune, there was a sudden sharp shout from up in the crow's nest.

The helmsman picked up his spy-glass. Charlie thought he saw smoke rising from the horizon.

As they drew nearer to the smoke, he could see that there was a galleon lying still in the water. Its main mast had snapped in twain, with the top half hanging off like a broken arm. Smoke drifted up from the stern, but he couldn't see any flames.

Captain Brock arrived on deck. He took a long

hard look at the scuppered vessel. It was flying the flag of St George.

'Looks like they're in trouble, Cap'n,' said Bosun Graham.

The Captain gave the matter some thought. 'Hmmm. Could be a trick. It has been known for pirates to fly false flags. I think it best we keep our distance. Circle it and let's see what we have here.'

The helmsman pulled to starboard and wheeled around it.

'Look Cap'n,' Charlie said. 'They're sending someone over.'

Someone was being lowered in a stretcher into a longboat.

'Looks like someone be dead,' said the Bosun. 'The face be covered. It don't bode well.'

'Stand steady,' said Captain Brock.

The boat approached. Eight sailors, wearing His Majesty's uniform, raised their oars, stood up and saluted. 'God save the King,' they chanted in unison.

'Permission to come aboard, Captain?' one of them asked. He had a mouthful of rotten teeth. Charlie didn't like the look of him, or the others.

'Hold fast,' said Captain Brock, 'what is your intention?'

Rotten-tooth pointed at the stretcher. 'Our captain here needs a surgeon.'

Captain Brock frowned. 'Where is your own surgeon?'

'He is dead, sir. We were attacked by pirates.'

The captain stared at the bundle. 'Why is he covered?'

'His face has been severely burned, sir.'

After giving it some thought, he invited them aboard, calling for Doctor Grimes, who suggested taking the victim below.

'Wait!' said the captain, curiosity getting the better of him. 'Let me take a look at him first.'

One of the passengers, Lady Fairfax, emerged from below deck.

'Is that man alright?' she enquired, just as the captain pulled the blanket aside. Instantly, she jumped back and let out a shriek.

The blanket flew in the air and a huge figure jumped to its feet, pushing Captain Brock to the deck, then grabbing Lady Fairfax around the neck.

She couldn't move an inch because her attacker's forearm was no ordinary forearm. It was a small cutlass, which by some strange mechanical device, was connected to the owner's elbow.

Lady Fairfax passed out but her attacker leaned back slightly and lifted her from the ground. He towered above her, at least six and a half feet tall. His face was that of a sneering skeleton. It was Blackheart.

He scanned the deck. 'Looks like we have a rum situation here, lads. I suggest you all drop your weapons.'

Captain Brock nodded and the men did as they were bid.

'Be seated,' Blackheart beckoned. He turned towards the captain. 'I would like you to assemble all your men on deck.'

'See to it,' ordered the Captain.

'I can't believe it's truly him,' Charlie whispered to Billy Griddle.

Blackheart's eyes darted towards him. 'Ah, I see we have a young 'un on board. Come here, lad.'

Charlie gulped and took a step back.

Catching everyone by surprise, the bosun snatched up a grappling hook and charged right at Blackheart, yelling, 'Die, you dastardly villain!'

It looked as if he was going to succeed in his assault but, at the last moment, and in the quickest of flashes, Blackheart unsheathed a dagger with his free arm and slashed it across the bosun's cheek. He fell to the floor, wincing in pain.

'Tut tut,' said Blackheart.

The eight men accompanying him made their way around the deck collecting weapons from the crew.

Blackheart's eyes focussed on Charlie again. 'Come here lad, I won't bite.'

Captain Brock caught Charlie's eye and shook his head.

Blackheart drew his blade gently across Lady Fairfax's neck. A dribble of blood seeped down onto her collar. A gasp went around the deck.

'Best do as he says,' said the captain.

Charlie made his way slowly forward, his heart beating like a snare drum. He stopped a few feet in front of the monstrous pirate, tilting his head right back to look up into his eyes.

As swift as lightning, Blackheart released Lady Fairfax, reached out and snatched up Charlie as a replacement, his blade-arm now resting on Charlie's shoulder.

'Who are you? What do you want?' one of the crew called out.

Blackheart laughed. 'Who am I? Who am I? I take offence at your ignorance. I am the Terror of the Seven Seas, the Scourge of the Caribbean. My name is Captain Carver Jones.'

Captain Brock spoke. 'I have heard of you, treacherous dog. I demand that you leave my vessel.'

Blackheart sneered. 'You do not find yourself in a position to make demands.'

'What do you want, scurvy villain?'

He smiled. 'Isn't it obvious? To put it simply, I want your ship. I will also be requiring some of your crew. Our numbers have been slightly depleted in recent encounters. Those who come with me will enjoy life on the high seas as buccaneers. Briny brethren all.'

The bosun spoke from his knees. 'We will not join you, you poxy cur.

Blackheart gave him the briefest of sideways glances, then sighed. 'Throw him overboard.'

Bosun Graham was dragged, kicking and yelling, to the side of the ship. With no hesitation, he was launched into thin air.

One of Blackheart's men, the one with the rotten teeth, stepped forward and addressed the crew. 'Raise your right arm if you would join us.'

After about half a minute of silence and no takers, a solitary hand went up, then two, then a few more.

Blackheart gave Charlie a little dig with his blade. 'What about you, me bucko?'

'I stand with Captain Brock,' said Charlie, proudly.

Blackheart shook his long, black hair. 'A sorry choice you have made, lad, and one you shall not live long to regret.'

Charlie noticed Jake Fletcher and Ned Sutton whispering together. Sharing a silent signal, they suddenly reached behind their backs, pulled out some pistols and aimed them at Blackheart's head.

In a flash, he unleashed a whip and disarmed both of them, slicing their hands in the process.

A dark look passed over his face as a cloud passed over the sun. 'I think we are in need of a demonstration of what befalls those who seek to oppose me.'

Ned was taken towards the mast and stripped to the waist.

'We need a drummer, I feel,' said Blackheart. He pushed Charlie to one side. With a whistle and a crack, he let fly with the whip, carving a slice in the deck. 'Let's see what kind of mood the cat is in today,' he grinned.

Charlie had seen crew members punished with Captain Brock's cat o' nine tails, which was nine knotted thongs of cotton cord, about two and a half feet long. Some crew referred to it as the Captain's daughter.

The monstrous and powerful thing that Blackheart held was leather, with tiny metal hooks attached to the ends of its thongs.

A protesting Ned was tied to the mast.

'Best not to look,' said Billy Griddle, but Charlie couldn't help himself. He put his hands over his face, but his fingers slid slowly apart.

There was a drum roll.

'Let this be a lesson to all of ye,' Blackheart announced, untangling some of the hooks and thongs.

Ned strained to see over his shoulder, his eyes open like oyster shells.

Blackheart pulled the whip back and released it with a snap.

Ned screamed like a banshee as a thin red line formed right across his back.

Blackheart swapped hands and unleashed the whip again. A fresh line formed, making a red criss-cross pattern on poor Ned's back.

One of Blackheart's men threw some seawater over the wounds and Ned passed out.

Nobody on board was expecting what happened next.

Blackheart pulled his arm back again. The whip began to glow – an odd underwater greenish colour.

With a quick stride forward, he let fly with it. There was no blood. There were no screams. What happened was even worse.

Ned sort of disintegrated. All that was left of him was a cloud of ash, which dispersed in the breeze and was gone.

A communal gasp swept across the deck.

Blackheart smiled and spun around slowly, his arms spread wide. 'Look on my works, be humbled and despair.'

Jake Fletcher, a look of horror on his face, made a break for it and dived overboard, choosing drowning over what he'd just witnessed.

Captain Brock shot forward, 'You evil cockroach, God shall pay you back for this.'

'God?' Blackheart laughed. 'The next man that moves will be tied to the end of this cannon. His demise will not be a pretty one. Now, who is with me?'

Not a soul moved.

Blackheart marched towards Billy Griddle. He sneered. 'What about you, old man?'

'I'm too old to be taking sides with the Devil,' said Billy. 'I'll not join your dirty crew.'

Blackheart's head went back. 'Strong words.' He spun around, his long coat-tails swishing behind him.

'Well then, let us see how you all manage without a captain.' He took out one of his pistols and pressed it against Captain Brock's temple.

The Captain looked resigned to his fate. 'Save yourselves, men.'

A plank was set out from the side of the ship, the final six feet of which extended over the water. Charlie had read stories about people being made to walk the plank but he had no notion that it actually happened.

Two of Blackheart's men chained a cannonball to the captain's feet.

'Why are they doing that?' asked Charlie.

'Ain't it obvious?' said Billy. 'So he sinks all the way down to the bottom of the briny.'

A defiant Captain Brock spat on Blackheart's coat and hissed, 'You shall be hanged.'

Blackheart exploded with laughter. 'That's been tried afore, on quite a few occasions.' He lowered his collar to reveal a series of rope-burn marks on his neck.

Billy surprised Charlie by pulling a dagger from under his sandal. He stood up and flung it, full force into Blackheart's chest. Blackheart stared at the protruding item, smiled, then simply pulled it out again. There was no blood.

'Brave effort, old man,' he smiled, 'but you cannot kill that which is already dead.' Sitting himself down on a barrel, he caught Charlie's eye and winked. He wiped his brow. 'Fetch me some grog, boy.'

'I'm not your servant,' said Charlie, defiantly.

'Fetch me some grog, or the old man goes on the cannon.'

'Best fetch him some,' said Billy. 'Bring him the special stuff.'

Charlie had no idea what Billy was talking about. Did he mean poison? Surely Blackheart would taste that.

'What are you two bilge-rats whispering about? Fetch me some grog, now. And no funny stuff, mind you. I can sniff treachery at twenty paces.'

'Special Recipe Grog,' whispered Billy, then winked.

Charlie headed down to the galley, closely followed by Rotten-tooth. He grabbed a bottle of rum from one of the shelves.

The waves outside grew higher and the ship tilted violently from side to side. Charlie felt the liquid in Grandma's recipe bottle sloshing around in his breeches pocket.

The ship made a sudden lurch and Rotten-tooth sprawled to the ground, letting fly with numerous curses.

Charlie had his back to the fallen pirate. He swiftly uncorked the recipe bottle, took a swig, without swallowing it and replaced it in his pocket. Then he uncorked the grog and emptied the contents of his mouth into it.

'You'd best not be drinking that grog,' called Rotten-tooth, pulling Charlie along with him.

They emerged on deck to the sight of Captain Brock standing precariously on the plank, holding a cannonball in his hands.

'Give me that,' ordered Blackheart. 'I thought perhaps you'd gone to Jamaica to fetch it.' He uncorked it and took a sniff. 'Hmm. Has a fine quality to it. My compliments to ye, Captain.'

Captain Brock, his brow beaded with perspiration, nearly lost his balance as a gust of wind suddenly picked up.

Blackheart took a huge swig, then let out a sigh. 'Tis a beautiful day,' he declared. 'That has warmed me up nicely.'

A look of confusion passed over him as his face began to change colour from ivory white to cherry pink. His right hand shot to his chest as he dropped the bottle. A stream of rum trickled its way across the deck.

'What have you done?' he gasped. 'What treachery is this?

He pulled his shirt open, the buttons flying from it. His skin was translucent. Plain for all to see, beneath his ribs, something throbbed.

A living, pulsing heart.

Blackheart roared like a Pacific typhoon, his eyes nearly popping out of their sockets.

'Kill him,' cried Captain Brock. 'He is mortal.'

Blackheart's men, paralyzed with shock, were

easily disarmed. They found themselves completely outnumbered.

Some of the crew charged at Blackheart but he bounded up onto the side-rail and, with the agility of a monkey, began climbing the rigging. A few climbed after him, daggers in their teeth. Charlie ran onto the plank to help guide Captain Brock back to safety.

'Well done, lad,' laughed Billy Griddle, slapping his thigh. 'You bested the Devil.'

Charlie was bewildered. 'How did you know the recipe would have that effect?'

Someone cried 'Watch out!'

Charlie glanced back over his shoulder to see Blackheart swinging towards him on a rope. He had no time to get out of the way. With a huge thud, he was flung backwards with Blackheart wrapped around him like a cocoon.

He plunged into the icy depths of the water, his breath stolen from him, he and his attacker sinking lower and lower into the depths. He felt long fingers around his neck, squeezing hard.

He was losing consciousness.

Then Blackheart's eyes, which were inches from his, suddenly stretched wide, as if they would pop out of his head. His mouth began to open and close frantically. Charlie thought he was trying to bite him. Abruptly and unexpectedly, Blackheart was snatched away, his body jerking from side to side like a dancing puppet.

Charlie burst through the water's surface, gasping for breath, a mad flurry of bubbles surrounding him. The water around him had turned crimson. A rope landed beside him. He reached for it, held on tight and was pulled to safety as a huge cheer erupted.

'What shall we do with these men, Captain?' Billy Griddle asked, pointing at Blackheart's crew.

The captain was about to speak when something strange happened. Blackheart's men began to age rapidly, decomposing and disintegrating before their eyes. Their ashes blew away in the breeze, as if they had never been real.

The next day, there was a service of thanksgiving.

It was decided that, once they reached port, the captain would find a new cabin boy and Charlie would become a fully-fledged member of the crew.

They even gave him a nickname – Braveheart.

CHAPTER SIX

SCARS

A brave heart was something I was now desperately in need of. Either that or martial arts expertise. Or both of them.

I helped Oliver slide his arms into the sleeves of his duffle coat. It was time for our weekly Saturday morning jaunt to the library. It was about a quarter of a mile to the library, a straight walk through the estate along Monnow Way.

It was pretty cold outside, with puddles still on the ground from yesterday's rain. I closed the front gate and off we headed, our next-door-neighbour's dog, Tillie, briefly following us.

Oliver spent virtually the whole journey bombarding me with knock-knock jokes, most of which I'd heard before:

'Knock knock.'

'Who's there?'

'A pile-up.'

'A pile-up who?'

Oliver found this hysterical.

We normally spend about half an hour in the library. Oliver can never make his mind up which books to choose. Sometimes he ends up with old favourites, books he's read many, many times before. Today, he chose three books, one about a lost owl, one about gardening pirates and one called, 'But I Don't Want to be a Pea.' I picked up 'The Hobbit' and the latest Michael Morpurgo.

The librarian, Julie, had a quick chat with us as we handed her our library cards. She was quite familiar with our Saturday morning routine.

As we stepped out under the library porch, I heard an all-too-familiar voice from above us. *'Oy, Four-eyes.'*

My heart skipped a beat. I spun around and looked up.

Oliver leaned across and whispered, 'They're not supposed to be up there.'

'I know.'

TJ was perched there, about eight feet off the ground, his legs dangling off the edge of the roof. A teenager sat next to him, cross-legged. Together, they resembled a pair of gargoyles.

TJ quickly manoeuvred himself and dropped down to the ground. Spiderman couldn't have done it any better.

'What poncy stuff have you got in there?' he said, snatching the carrier bag from my hand. Sneering, he sifted through the contents. 'Baby books.'

Oliver's eyes opened wide in horror.

'What are you staring at?' TJ laughed. 'Hey, he's even smaller than you.'

'He's five,' I said. 'Leave him alone.'

'Or what?'

'Or I'll kick you,' growled Oliver.

TJ laughed. 'He's a lot braver than you, Underpants.'

I could smell smoke. The teenager had a cigarette in his hand and a big plastic bottle of cider next to his leg. The local police-station was only a few metres away.

'Can we have our books back?' I said.

TJ casually dropped the carrier bag onto the floor, just missing a puddle.

'Why don't you kick his head in, bro?' the teenager called down. 'Ain't he the one who pushed your bag in the poo?'

So this was TJ's stepbrother, the notorious Jordan Bates.

TJ shook his head. 'He's not worth it.'

He gave me a gentle push. '*Are* you?'

Before I could stop him, Oliver scuttled towards TJ and booted him on the shin. Instinctively, TJ pushed him away. Oliver lost his balance and fell onto his rear end.

I didn't hesitate. Nobody hurts my little brother. I charged straight at TJ and tackled him to the floor. After a bit of a tussle, TJ emerged on top, sitting on my chest.

'Leave my big brother alone,' Oliver called out. He started punching TJ's arms.

'Big?' laughed TJ.

I couldn't budge. He was a dead weight.

Jordan leaned forward over the edge of the porch roof. 'Give him a slap, Teej.'

TJ gave me a few playful slaps across the cheeks, then pressed his palm, quite hard, into my face so that I couldn't breathe.

'Looks like he's crying,' said Jordan.

TJ suddenly scrambled to his feet. Somebody was heading towards us. An old lady.

My temper was up. I got to my feet and flew at him, windmill arms flailing. Surprisingly, he gave me his back and moved away from me, using one arm to protect the back of his head.

The old lady called out, 'Oy, you two!!'

I couldn't stop, though. It felt so good to be the one with the power for a change.

Jordan broke out into hyena-like laughter. 'Hey, bro, he's kicking your butt!'

I momentarily lost concentration and momentum. Taking advantage of this, TJ swung his arm back, full force. His fist connected with my nose. I felt a tingling sensation right across my face. My eyes began to water of their own accord and then my nose started to bleed.

An abrupt, percussive banging sound came from the library window. It was Julie.

Jordan clambered quickly down to the ground and he and TJ ran for it, nearly causing an accident as they shot across the road.

Julie came out to see what was going on. She ushered us inside and held the bridge of my nose until it stopped bleeding. Oliver looked traumatized, so she gave him some Haribos.

'I know those boys,' she said. 'They've been banned from here.'

On the way back, Oliver couldn't shut up about the fight. 'Why did you let him hit you, Charlie? You weren't crying really, were you? I know you could beat him if you tried.'

I had a serious headache and Oliver's voice was beginning to grate. I tried to ignore him but the questions kept coming, like a dripping tap. My nerves were raw.

I came to a sudden halt, grabbed hold of his arm, shook him and yelled at the top of my voice. 'Will you just shut up! Shut up, shut up, SHUT UP!!'

I regretted it immediately. Oliver looked like a rabbit frozen in the headlights.

A postman emerged from behind a hedge. He stared at me, tutted and shook his head. 'That's no way to treat your brother, is it?' He bent down to Oliver's level. 'Are you okay, little man?'

Oliver nodded, tears streaming down his cheeks.

'Look, you've scared him.'

I grabbed Oliver's hand. ' Come on. Let's go.'

The postman stood and watched us a bit longer. He tutted again, then moved on.

When we arrived home, Mum spotted the dried

blood on my nose and wanted to know all about it. She fetched the telephone directory and was on the verge of phoning TJ's parents, but I begged her not to, virtually pulling the phone out of her hands. 'It won't do any good. It'll only make things worse.'

Noticing my obvious distress, she put the phone down. 'Well, I'll be letting Miss Cashman know on Monday morning. This is just not happening again.'

*

I laughed in frustration when Miss Cashman announced in assembly on Monday morning that this week was anti-bullying week. Why couldn't *every* week be anti-bullying week?

Back in class, Mr Brock got the ball rolling straight away. He read a poem called 'He pushed her.' It started like this:

Harry pushed her;
He pushed her around;
He pushed his sister.
Before school, after school;
On weekends.
He pushed his sister.

It was quite a clever poem because we all assumed that the poem was about a boy bullying his sister but it turned out that the sister was disabled and the boy was actually *helping* her by pushing her around in a wheelchair.

'Hands up if you think you've ever been the victim of bullying,' Mr Brock said.

My hand went up without hesitation, followed by about three quarters of the class. I was quite surprised by some of the hands in the air.

TJ's hands stayed firmly on his desk. He was busy drawing what looked like a planet-destroying robot.

Sir nodded in agreement. 'Yes, unfortunately, it happens to a lot of people. Even grown-ups. Now, let's switch it over. Hands up if you've ever bullied anyone else. In other words, *you've* been the bully. Now, be honest, all of you.'

Not one hand went up. A few people exchanged nervous glances.

Sir shook his head and laughed. 'I see, so three quarters of you have been bullied, but nobody is doing the bullying. That's strange, isn't it? Think back over the last seven years in school. Has there ever been someone you didn't particularly like and you were maybe a bit horrible towards him or her and you made their life miserable?'

With a bit of hesitation, a few hands went up. Perhaps a quarter of the class. TJ carried on drawing his robot, which looked like it was biting the heads off some tiny alien creatures.

'That's more like it,' said Sir. 'Thanks for your honesty. Because how can we expect to stop bullying if we don't recognize the bully in ourselves? I'm sure

I've probably bullied someone at some stage in my life. Maybe, sometimes, I accidentally do it as a teacher.'

None of this was much help to me in my current situation. TJ didn't appear to be paying the slightest attention to the discussion. He might as well have not been in the room.

I noticed Mr Brock giving some sort of signal to Mr Jackson. He grabbed the pencil from TJ. Huffing and puffing, TJ folded his arms.

'What types of bullying are there?' asked Sir. 'What does bullying look like?'

'People being beaten up,' said Ieuan.

'Yes, Ieuan,' Sir nodded, 'that's called physical bullying. Punching, kicking, generally hurting. But is that the worst kind of bullying?'

Half the class nodded vigorously.

Sir opened up a Power-point slide. In big letters were the words

STICKS AND STONES MAY BREAK MY BONES
BUT NAMES WILL NEVER HURT ME

'Have a look at that. Is it true?'

Everyone nodded. A classroom full of nodding dogs.

'Really?' said Sir. 'Have a think about it. Put your hand up if you've ever been called names that you didn't much like.'

Quite a few hands went up.

'What kinds of things have you been called?

'Four-eyes,' I said. 'Underpants. Midget.'

'But you *are* a midget,' said TJ, suddenly waking up. 'How is that bullying?'

'Perhaps he doesn't like it,' said Mr Brock.

'I can't help that,' said TJ.

Other kids in the class admitted to having been called, at various times, Fatty, Skinny, Spotty, Dweeb and Gingernut.

There were a few giggles. Sir silenced the gigglers with a stern look until they were quiet.

'Is it true, then,' asked Sir, 'that names don't hurt?'

'No,' I said, with conviction.

'Exactly, Charlie. They *do* hurt. It's called verbal bullying. Some people think it's worse than physical bullying. Words can be as sharp as knives, as vicious as bullets.'

'How can a name be worse than a punch in the face?' laughed TJ. He just didn't get it.

Mr Brock took a deep breath. 'Has anyone ever called you names, TJ?'

'Hah, they wouldn't dare.' He paused, then mumbled, as a sort of after-thought. 'Well, in my house everyone calls me stupid. But that's quite funny. I am pretty stupid.'

Sir gave us all a blank piece of A4 paper each and asked us to stand up. TJ remained seated.

'Now, I know this may appear strange, but when I say 'Go', I want you to shout at your piece of paper, call it names, crumple it up, stamp on it. Just don't rip it.'

TJ stood up. This was now *his* kind of game.

Sir shouted, 'Go,' and suddenly the classroom became very loud. Twenty-five pieces of paper were given the rough treatment for about twenty seconds.

'Now,' said Sir, 'I want you to open up your piece of paper, which should still be in one piece. I want you to say sorry to it.'

With a few giggles, we did as we were told.

'What do you notice about your piece of paper?' Sir asked us.

'It needs ironing,' said Ryan.

'It's got scars all over it,' said Shannon.

'Exactly,' said Sir. 'Even though you've apologized and even though your piece of paper is still in one piece, you can see how badly scarred it is. And it won't be easy to get rid of those scars, will it?'

We all nodded. Most of us had got the point. TJ's piece of paper looked as if it had been chewed up by a wild animal.

Mr Brock showed us some poems that children had written, about what it feels like to be bullied. One victim said he felt like a tiny island surrounded by a deep dark ocean full of sharks. Another said she felt like an empty swing in a deserted playground.

'So why do bullies bully? Talk to your partner.'

'Because they're jealous of someone else?' offered Shannon.

'Can you give me an example?'

'Well, you might have something they haven't got. Like, maybe, a Cath Kidston bag.'

I had no idea what that was.

'Some people bully to make themselves look big,' said Ryan.

'I think bullies are just mean,' offered Emily.

'Perhaps I'm naïve,' Sir said, 'but I don't think that people are naturally mean and horrible. Bullying is about power. Exerting power over other people. Usually, bullies have very little power in their own lives. They are often bullied by parents or older siblings so they take it out on weaker people. It's a vicious cycle.' He paused and threw a glance at TJ. 'How can we stop it? What should you do if you are being bullied?'

I listened to the list of answers in frustration: tell an adult or a friend, call Childline, put a note in the bully box, ignore it, try not to show you're upset or angry, don't fight back, give the bully what they want, make a joke of it, avoid being in isolated places, keep a diary. As far as I was concerned, they were a load of old pants.

'What should we do to bullies?' Sir asked.

I knew what I wanted. I wanted TJ to get a taste of his own medicine. To know what it was like to be a victim. To step into *my* shoes for a while.

In Sir's opinion, bullies needed educating. Basically, we should talk to them, understand what makes them tick, try and persuade them to change.

No help whatsoever.

A strange feeling came over me.

I got up and headed towards the classroom door.

'Charlie?' said a puzzled Mr Brock.

'I need the toilet,' I said.

'Ask first, please.'

'May I go to the toilet?'

I didn't wait for an answer. I felt like a ticking time-bomb.

CHAPTER SEVEN

BUGGED

I carried my bad mood into the afternoon with me. To make matters worse, we had DT, my absolutely least favourite subject.

Mr Jones takes us for DT once a fortnight in his special Art/Design and Technology room, so that Mr Brock can have some planning and marking time. Mr Jones has been in the school for donkeys' years. He's even taught some of my classmates' mums and dads. He comes from Llanelli and he speaks Welsh to us and supports the Scarlets.

He's quite an unusual looking guy, with salt-and-pepper curly hair, a big bushy moustache and a serious tan. His hands are huge and full of scars, cuts and bruises. I'm slightly scared of him, to be honest. He has a good sense of humour but, when he loses his temper, he's totally volcanic. According to rumours, he actually swears when he really loses it. Not the *F-bomb,* of course, but the *sh* word and a few of the *b* words.

I'm not great at making things and fixing things. I am much, much better at imagining things. My designs are normally okay, but the finished models never exactly turn out the way I want them to.

We'd been making buggies for the last few sessions, using wooden frames and plastic wheel and powered by batteries, worm gears and cog-wheels.

As I moped into the DT room, I noticed that Mr Jones had set out our models ready for us, so that we could get started straight away. He was standing at the sink in his long, grey workshop-coat, slurping from a huge mug of tea. It smelled like he'd just had a secret fag too.

'Morning! *Bore da,* Charlie. *Popeth yn iawn?* Everything alright?' he enquired, half-smiling, half-frowning.

I nodded.

Ieuan's buggy sat next to mine on the workbench. It didn't look half as good as mine but I knew it would work better. Adjacent to our models was a black buggy with a plastic devil stuck to the top of it and what looked like a pitchfork jutting out of the front.

'Whose is that?' Ieuan whispered.

'His,' I pointed, as TJ swaggered into the room.

'*Bore da!* Morning, TJ,' smiled Mr Jones.

TJ gave him a bit of a smile back, and a thumbs-up. DT is *his* favourite subject.

As we were now all in, Mr Jones emptied the remains of his tea into the sink and swilled out his mug. '*Nawrte.* Right-oh,' he announced, 'I don't really want to waste a lot of time nattering. As most of you have completed the designing and making process, your next step is to add some finish to your models.

Anyone who manages to get that done today can fill out an evaluation sheet. All clear?'

Lots of nods.

'Right, I'll leave you to it, then. If you come across any problems you can't resolve... then try harder. You need to learn to persevere. Resilience, isn't that *right*, Charlie?'

I jumped slightly. 'Yes sir.'

He left us to it.

I made my way to the resources area and got myself some newspaper, a brush, some red paint and white paint and then headed to the sink to fetch some water.

I couldn't help staring at TJ's buggy as I came back.

Unfortunately, TJ spotted the look. 'What's *your* problem?'

'Nothing,' I said. 'I was just wondering what *that* was for.' I pointed at the pitchfork.

He ignored me.

Ieuan looked up, curious. 'What *is* it for?'

'To kill nosey-parkers,' mumbled TJ, heading off to get some paint.

'Oh.'

'He's a psycho,' Ieuan whispered.

A few minutes later, TJ returned with a paint palette, all six compartments of which were filled with black.

'Sure you've got enough paint there?' Ieuan laughed.

TJ scowled.

'Aren't you gonna use any other colours, then?' Ieuan asked him in all innocence.

'Does it look like?'

TJ stared at my buggy. 'I'm amazed you're not using pink, Four-eyes. Pink's your colour, isn't it?'

I wasn't in the mood for him. I didn't see why *I* had to be picked on all the time. It wouldn't have taken much for me to pick up his model and throw it at him, pitchfork first.

'Bet yours doesn't even move,' said TJ, pouring on the scorn.

'Yes it does. Does *yours*?'

The next thing I knew, little black flecks of paint appeared all over my buggy, as if it was raining oil or something.

I glanced up. TJ was casually applying paint to his model. He had a smirk pinned to his face. 'Oops, sorry,' he said, 'my hand must have slipped.'

Mr Jones arrived on the scene. 'What's up?' he enquired.

'Nothing sir,' said TJ, the picture of innocence, 'my brush accidentally flicked away from my hand, that's all.'

'Liar,' I snapped.

Mr Jones raised both his palms. 'Hey, hey, *digon*! Enough now boys! Take it easy. Don't spoil it now. You're doing some good work here.' He paused. 'Why don't you try them out?'

There was a narrow, corridor-like, desk-free space

at one side of the classroom. Mr Jones had set it aside specially for trials.

Sir left us to think about it and headed off towards another group.

'That's a laugh,' sneered TJ. 'Like yours is gonna actually work. A fiver says mine beats yours any day of the week.'

I was all fired up. 'You're on,' I said.

Ieuan agreed to be witness to the bet. He grabbed a metre stick to use as a finishing line and knelt down about five metres away from us.

TJ and I hunkered down behind our buggies, fingers on switches.

'After three?' Ieuan suggested.

'*On* three or *after* three?' said TJ, awkward as ever.

'After three, as in one two three *go.*'

'Right.'

Ieuan counted and the race was on. The buggies lurched into life. Mine shot into an early lead, one of its front wheels wobbling, but TJ's quickly overtook it, leaving a trail of black paint in its wake.

'Woooo-hooo!' he yelled, his demon-buggy now a dead cert to win. But then he could only watch, goggle-eyed, as the vehicle appeared to grow a mind of its own and veered off somewhere to the left. He set off after it, but failed to catch it. It disappeared under a desk and then headed straight into an open metal cupboard. A lone strip of dowelling rod rolled off the top shelf and bounced off the top of it.

Meanwhile, tortoise-like, my machine tottered over the finishing line. I couldn't help but smirk.

TJ looked on, open-mouthed and helpless, as the falling dowelling rod was swiftly followed by the rest of its family. With a clatter and a crunch, a whole avalanche of them came raining down on top of his model.

I had to stop myself saying 'Oops.' Instead, I reminded TJ of the fiver he now owed me.

TJ's clenched fists throbbed like two beating hearts. 'I'm gonna kill you!'

'What the heck's going on now?' shouted Mr Jones, running over.

'It was an accident, sir,' Ieuan explained.

TJ started pulling the dowelling rods off his buggy and flinging them behind him, willy-nilly, with no concern for where they were landing.

'Hey, hey!' said Sir, his arm on TJ's shoulders to restrain him.

TJ managed to retrieve his buggy. The pitchfork at the front had snapped off, two of the wheels were now horizontal and there was a crack down the middle of the chassis. He dangled it in his hand as if it was a dead pet.

With a look of grave concern, Mr Jones walked over to the cupboard and examined the top shelf to see if anything else was loose. This was now a major health and safety incident.

'I know you're upset, TJ,' he said, 'but accidents happen.'

TJ strode towards the finishing line. 'Yeah,' he said, 'I know they do – like *this*.' He lifted his foot and, with full force, stomped on my buggy.

There was a tremendous crack, two of the wheels shot off in opposite directions and the chassis dropped in the middle, like a sunken flan.

Owen Jarrett, who had just nipped out to the toilet, chose entirely the wrong moment to walk back into the room.

'What's up, guys?' he said.

And then TJ stomped on my buggy again.

I wasn't smiling any more. I'd spent hours making the blasted thing. Something bad was going to happen, I could feel it.

With unexpected strength, I ran at TJ and pushed him away from the wreckage. He pushed me straight back and stomped on the buggy for a third time. There was now nothing left of it. It looked like a piece of modern art.

I couldn't stop myself. My blood was boiling. I lowered my head and charged towards TJ, head first, slamming into his chest and sending him flying backwards. He lost his balance and went sprawling towards the metal cupboard. Contact was made. The cupboard wobbled precariously. For one awful second I thought the whole thing was going to fall on him. Instead, the middle shelf tilted forward abruptly and two trays full of cogs and wheels emptied themselves all over TJ and the floor.

Mr Jones did not look amused.

TJ leapt to his feet, scattering dowelling like raw spaghetti and headed straight for me.

Sir managed to step in between the two of us. 'Oy, oy, calm it down, the two of you, calm it down. Enough!!'

Meanwhile, some of the fallen wheels continued to travel around the room.

Mr Brock appeared in the open doorway. He clearly couldn't believe the scene that confronted him. 'Everything all right, Mr Jones?' he asked.

'No, not really,' said a red-faced Mr Jones. 'I've got these two clowns here trying to turn this place into a wrestling ring.'

Mr Brock looked flustered. 'Oh... uh... right... Miss Cashman would like to see TJ. Do you mind if I take him?'

'Take him, take him,' said Mr Jones, releasing his hold.

'I'll see you later,' TJ snarled at me as he was led away.

'Not if I see you first!' I yelled back.

Now would be a good time to discover that I had secret superpowers.

CHAPTER EIGHT

GO CHARLIE GO

I had the weirdest dream that night. Normally, when you dream, if you remember any of it at all, you only remember bits of it and it all seems a bit random, but I dreamed a whole story, from beginning to end.

The superhero thing must have been playing on my mind because that's what it was about. I started writing it down in my notebook as soon as I woke up and carried on with it on the bus

I finished it that evening and read it to Oliver and his best friend, Louis, who was sleeping over. Louis is not the best listener in the world, being even more hyperactive than Oliver. The two of them sat side-by-side in Oliver's bed, one wearing Transformers pyjamas, the other dressed as Spiderman.

I sat forward and began:

Charlie Underwood didn't exactly look like a superhero.

'That's *your* name,' Louis frowned.

I nodded.

'You're not a superhero.'

I raised my eyebrows. 'It's called pretend.'

He was unusually small for his age, he wore round glasses and had skin as pale as milk.

Some of the other, bigger, stronger boys in his class looked like maybe they could possibly be secret superheroes, but definitely not Charlie. He enjoyed reading about superheroes though, like the Incredible Hulk with his huge, green muscles and bad temper; the Amazing Spiderman who could shoot webs out of his hands and use them to swing from skyscraper to skyscraper; Batman with his cool Bat-mobile; Daredevil, Iron Man, Thor, the Fantastic Four, the X-Men, even Captain Underpants.

'Kapow!' yelled Louis, nearly elbowing Oliver in the face.

I gave him my best fake-smile.

Charlie wasn't brave or strong like them. He was as quiet and timid as a mouse. So quiet you'd hardly notice he was there. Mr Brock often marked him absent in the register, even though he was actually in school.

At playtimes, Charlie liked to imagine he was a superhero – Charlie Underwood, Wonderboy! Some kid would throw a ball, it would roll under one of the teachers' cars and Charlie would picture himself bounding over and lifting up the vehicle with his little finger, while someone else dived under to retrieve it. Or he would notice someone being bullied and he would imagine the cheesy Quavers he was holding were magic missiles which he could fire at the bullies and make them shrink to the size of cowardly weasels.

'I like Quavers,' said Oliver.

'Me too,' said Louis, chomping invisible crisps.

Or he would imagine the school secretary running out of fruit to sell for morning break. She would plead, 'Be a darling, Charlie, nip to the shop and get some more.' Quick as a flash, he would throw on his cape and rocket along Monnow Way to Bettws Shopping Centre and acquire those urgently needed apples, oranges and bananas.

One day, Charlie Underwood made a mistake. A big mistake. He was standing on the yard near Barnaby, the bear-shaped bin, talking to some of the boys in his class about how great the new 'Iron Man' DVD was, when he heard himself say, out loud, ' Nobody knows this, but I'm a secret superhero.'

'What did you say?' laughed Deri Davies.

'Nothing,' said Charlie. But it was too late. The words had escaped from his lips. Soon the whole school knew that Charlie Underwood thought he was a superhero. In other words, he was nuts.

'What's your superpower, then?' Gareth Whitehead enquired. 'All superheroes have special powers. The Hulk is super-strong, Superman can fly, Mr Fantastic is stretchy, Iron Man has his armour. What about you? What can you do?'

Charlie looked down at his trainers. 'I don't know,' he muttered.

''Course you don't know,' said Gareth, "cos you ain't got any special powers!'

'Yes I have,' said Charlie.

Gareth snorted and grabbed hold of one of Charlie's arms. 'Can you rip a double-decker bus in half with your big biceps, then?'

'No,' said Charlie.

'Can you make yourself invisible and go and spy on the girls?'

'No.'

'Can you fly to Cwmbran and back in five seconds?'

'No.' A tear formed in Charlie's eye.

'Then you're not a superhero, are you?' said Gareth, patting Charlie on the head. 'And you need to get a new brain for Christmas. Anyway, superheroes don't cry.'

'I'm not crying,' said Charlie.

'I don't like those other boys,' said Oliver. 'They're nasty.'

'Biff!' said Louis, punching his own palm.

'Watch the milk,' I said. Two glasses of milk were perched on the bedside cabinet, next to the lamp.

While all this was going in, somebody, not too far away, was listening. Not some-body, exactly. Something. Something lying at the bottom of the canal.

Nobody knew about the existence of this thing, this creature. If they suspected, they would all have moved away, as far away as possible. Nobody would be living in Bettws any more.

'Is it a monster?' asked Oliver.

'Yes.'

'Is it the Whomper Whoomper Snicker Snacker?'

'No,' I laughed.

'What's the Whomper Whoomper Snicker Snacker?' asked Louis.

'Never mind,' I said.

This secretive and sneaky creature was called Karvrog.

'Karvrog? That's a funny name.'

Karvrog lived in a little tunnel just off the canal but, most days, he liked to lie under the water and spy on people walking by. Hundreds of years ago, he used to live in a damp cave in Brecon, but then somebody built the canal. One day, he slid into it and followed it all the way through Abergavenny and Crickhowell and Pontypool and Cwmbran. He found a spot he liked just between two villages called Malpas and Bettws.

It was quiet and peaceful, until somebody built a school nearby. He hated noise, having very sensitive ears. Break-times and dinner-times were an absolute nightmare to him.

Sometimes, people out walking or jogging would be aware of strange bubbles rising to the surface of the canal and they would hear a noise that sounded like a burp. Owen Jarrett said he saw a pair of eyes once, peering from behind a shopping trolley which someone had thrown into the canal. It felt as though someone was watching him, he said, and scooted home as fast as his little legs would carry him.

Karvrog listened to the yelling and the laughing of the children on the yard. The noises they made infuriated him. It sounded as if a hundred seagulls were squawking and screeching inside his head. He pressed his claws over his ears and crouched into a ball on the bottom of the canal bed. He had to make it stop. Enough was enough.

He slithered out of the canal, down a steep bank and into the brook. He followed it as it wound its way towards a tall wire-fence.

He stood up, if you could call it that, for he couldn't really stand up properly. He crouched. Black all over, with rubbery skin, his legs were bendy, his feet were flippered like a frog's and his arms were monkey-long. His pot belly made him look as though he'd swallowed a basketball. On top of his head sat a row of spikes, just like you might see on a hedgehog or a porcupine. His eyes were very large and looked as if they might pop out at you at any moment. They were constantly on the move, darting from side to side.

'He's ugly.'

'Uh-huh.'

His mouth was wide and, protruding from it was a pair of elephant-like tusks, which curved downwards instead of up. He had a long raspy tongue which flopped around like a dead snake. His breathing was laboured and heavy, as if he had asthma.

The noise of the children playing made his brain rattle. With one giant leap, he bounded over the fence and landed with a squelch right in front of Owen Jarrett, who screamed like a girl. Karvrog's tongue shot out and grabbed him by the ankle. Owen's left shoe slid off and he hobbled into the building, faster than the Road Runner.

'MEEP MEEP,' said Louis.

The yard went quiet. The only sounds were the leaves rustling on the trees, a few birds singing and the drone of a jet high up in the sky. All the children and grown-ups had now spotted the creature. They froze in horror.

Karvrog smiled grotesquely and hopped towards three Y6 girls, Emily, Shannon and Seren, who slowly backed up towards the fence. He left a trail of slime behind him. He jabbered away to himself, but not in any language recognizable to human beings.

'What is that?' gasped Mrs Reilly, one of the dinner supervisors.

'I have no idea,' said Miss Tutton, 'but let's get the kids inside, quick!'

Gareth and Deri shot past Charlie like a pair of cheetahs on skates.

'Wait!' Charlie cried.

'You wait!' said Gareth. 'We're off!!'

'But what about the girls?'

'Why don't you go and rescue them, Mr Superhero?' said Deri. 'Good luck and goodbye.'

Charlie closed his eyes. He felt kind of tingly all over. He knew his big moment had arrived.

'Here goes,' he said to himself as he marched across the yard towards the large creature, which was staring intently at the three girls and making some extremely odd noises.

Charlie stood directly behind Karvrog, fists resting on his hips. He cleared his throat and yelled at the top of his voice, 'Oy you, let them go!' His voice echoed right across the yard.

'Let them go, you bad monster!!' yelled Louis.

Oliver's eyes peeped above the quilt cover.

The creature's head swivelled around. Its mouth opened wide like a huge, wet cave. It let out an ear-piercing screech, a sound like fingernails being scraped down a blackboard. Its eyes had become extra large. Charlie could see its heart beating in its chest. It was not in a good mood.

But it chose to ignore him, turning away from him and moving even closer to the three girls. They sobbed and turned their backs to it, grabbing onto the fence.

'I said, let them go!' insisted Charlie.

This time, Karvrog didn't even bother turning around.

Charlie took his glasses off and rubbed them clean. Then he hooked them back on and began to concentrate intently on the creature's back. He mumbled to himself 'Go Charlie go. Go, Charlie go.'

'What's he doing?' said Deri Davies.

Gareth Whitehead frowned. 'Looks like he's talking to himself.'

'Get over here, Charlie,' Mrs Reilly called over to him, but he was so focussed he didn't even hear her. Placing his fingers on his temples, he stared intensely at the creature's back.

To everyone's amazement, two thin beams of red light shot out from his eyes and hit Karvrog on the butt. The creature yelped and shot about ten feet in the air. As it landed, Charlie hit him again with the laser beams, this time on the back of his neck. Like a ricocheting bullet, Karvrog bounced off towards the field, howling and shrieking along the way.

Louis thought this was the funniest thing ever and began rolling around laughing. I had to catch him before he fell off the bed.

Emily, Shannon and Seren scooted towards safety as the rest of the yard clapped and cheered. Karvrog placed his claws over his ears and began to roll around on the ground in pain.

Meanwhile, Mrs Reilly and Miss Tutton led the children off the yard and into the hall.

Unfortunately, two boys from Reception, Oliver and Louis, were dawdling and didn't notice they were the only children left outside. Oliver was picking his nose and Louis was admiring his new Captain America lunchbox.

'Oliver and Louis, that's us!' said Oliver.

'We're in the story, we're in the story,' chanted Louis, bouncing up and down.

'What's that noise?' Mum called from downstairs.

'It's okay!' I called back.

Mrs Reilly ran towards the two boys, but Karvrog had already spotted them and lolloped over towards them, licking his lips. Louis didn't seem to understand that the creature was dangerous. 'Hello,' he said, smiling at it. Oliver looked puzzled.

'RUN!!' shrieked Mrs Reilly, but they ignored her.

Charlie Underwood had an idea. Bending his legs slightly, he reached out and spread his arms around as much of Barnaby the Bin as he could.

'What's he doing now?' said Deri, biting his nails.

Gareth shook his head in disbelief. 'Looks like he's hugging Barnaby the bin.'

But he wasn't hugging it. Unbelievably, even though it was as tall as he was and twice as wide, he managed to lift it off the ground. He spun around with it as if he were dancing with it. Faster and faster, like a mini-tornado, he twisted and twisted.

Then, abruptly, he let it go.

Some people put their hands over their eyes. It looked for one minute as if the bin might actually land on the two little boys and squish them. 'Look out!' someone shrieked.

Oliver and Louis spun around, saw the flying bear-bin shooting towards them and ducked. It skimmed past their heads and hit Karvrog right in the chops.

Oliver burst out laughing. Louis cheered like a wrestling fan.

It sent him topsy-turvy, helter-skelter, head-over-heels. Like an oversized bowling ball, he rolled from one end of the field to the other. The boys hurtled towards the safety of the hall as quickly as they could. But Louis tripped and stumbled over his laces.

Karvrog screeched like a banshee. His breathing became heavier, as if he was going to explode.

But he didn't explode. He grew. Bigger. Bigger. Bigger.

Until he was the size of a car.

'That's really big,' said Oliver, looking worried.

With one huge bound, he landed right in front of five-year-old Louis, blocking his escape route entirely.

'*Go away you big fat monster!*' *said Louis, poking his tongue out at it.*

I took a sip of Diet Pepsi. Oliver and Louis took sips of their milk, giving themselves white moustaches.

Karvrog was not impressed. His long, thick, purple tongue shot out and wrapped itself around his victim, pulling him along the ground.

Charlie Underwood couldn't get there fast enough to prevent it happening. 'Let him go, you bully!' he called out.

The creature ignored him.

Without hesitation, Charlie took a packet of cheesy Quavers from his jacket pocket and opened them up.

'What's he doing now?' said Deri Davies, frowning.

'Looks like he's having a snack,' said Gareth.

'This is no time for food,' said Deri, shaking his head in disbelief.

Charlie held his hand out, palm facing upwards, a little Quaver resting on top of it, wobbling in the breeze. He concentrated and focussed with all his might.

Chanting broke out around him: 'Go Charlie go! Go Charlie go! Go...'

Charlie blew hard. Really hard and really quick. The Quaver shot from his hand as fast as a bullet and hit Karvrog on his well-exposed tongue. It sizzled like a sausage in a pan. He howled in agony and wriggled around but still didn't let go of Louis.

Charlie took three more Quavers out of the packet and blew them in quick succession. Rat-a-tat-tat.

Karvrog's tongue instantly broke out in angry red spots. He could no longer bear the pain. He released the boy, his tongue slithering swiftly back into the safe cave of his mouth. Louis scampered off like a little rabbit.

Howling like a wolf caught in a trap, Karvrog began to grow.

'Will you look at that?' Shannon pointed. The creature was now the size of a mini-bus.

'Oh my goodness, oh my goodness!' cried Emily. 'It's heading for Charlie. What's gonna happen now?'

Charlie didn't look bothered at all.

Karvrog looked angry and confused. Why was this boy so calm? Why wasn't he scared out of his wits?

Charlie just stood there, casually munching. 'Mmmmm,' he said. 'Yummylicious!'

Mrs Reilly let out a little gasp. 'Look, he's getting bigger!'

'Who, the monster?' said Miss Tutton.

'No, not the monster. Charlie! Look!'

It was true. Taller and taller Charlie grew. Stronger and stronger, with muscles like a WWF wrestler.

His school clothes fell away from him, revealing a superhero costume underneath. Red, green and white, the colours of the Welsh flag. There was a picture of a red dragon on his chest. He ate some more Quavers until he was even taller than Mrs Lewis.

'Go Charlie go!' all the children and teachers chanted, stomping their feet, and banging on the windows.

Charlie turned around, winked at them and gave them the thumbs up sign.

'That's my big brother,' declared Oliver Underwood.

Karvrog shook his head furiously. Spit and slobber flew everywhere. He let out a huge burp and stretched wide his manhole sized mouth. He was fed up with this Charlie Underwood creature. He was going to gobble him up.

To everyone's surprise, Charlie retreated towards the fence.

'I knew it,' said Gareth. 'He's chickening out.'

Karvrog stayed where he was for a moment. He was totally bewildered. One minute the boy wanted to fight, the next he was running away.

To the dinner supervisors' horror, Charlie commenced ripping down the wire fence that separated the yard from the Community Centre. It was ten feet tall at least, and there was a lot of it. With one end of it in his hand and the other end trailing behind him like a wedding dress, he began to zoom around Karvrog, faster and faster, at a dizzying speed.

'OMG!' gasped Gareth. 'He's flying!'

'I can't see him!' said Deri. 'He's a blur!'

In no time at all, before you could even say 'What's occurring?' Charlie had used the fence-wire as a net and wrapped Karvrog up in a big roll. The creature became frenzied in its attempt to escape but it was tied up tighter than a Thanksgiving turkey.

Charlie flew around for a bit, then came down to land. He shrank back down to his normal size and took a puff of his inhaler.

After an epic struggle against the net, Karvrog tired himself out completely. He was pooped.

Within minutes, the police and fire service arrived on the scene and cordoned off the area. They called for the local vet, who gave the creature an injection to make him unconscious. They took him away in a big truck.

When it was all clear, the children came running out onto the yard. Some of the Year Six boys hoisted Charlie onto their shoulders and gave him a much-deserved lap of honour.

Everyone chanted at the top of their voices, 'Go, Charlie, go!!'

Charlie's smile couldn't have been any wider.

'What happened to Karvrog?' asked Oliver.

Well, scientists and zoologists studied him for a while and came to the conclusion he was harmless, as long as he had plenty of peace and quiet. They decided to put him on a ship and take him to live in a secluded rainforest in South America, where there would be no screaming children to bother him. He didn't have a particularly good time at first because of all the screeching birds and howling monkeys. Eventually, though, he found a nice dark cave and lived happily ever after. Sort of.

CHAPTER NINE

PUSHOVER

Thankfully, I didn't need superpowers just yet. Mr Brock, now more fully aware of the TJ situation, seemed to be looking out for me.

He'd arranged for us to go to St Fagan's National History Museum for our end-of-year class trip. I'd been a few times before with my mum and dad. I quite liked looking at all the old houses and farms and churches. You could almost imagine yourself going back in time as you walked around them.

TJ had obviously never heard of St Fagan's. Ever since Sir had told us where we'd be going, he'd kept referring to our destination as St Faggots.

I sat by myself on the outward journey, gazing at the passing scenery and eavesdropping on a conversation between Mr Brock and TJ, who sat two seats in front of me. I was astonished that TJ had been allowed to come. He was basically a walking health and safety hazard.

'So, what kind of things do you do in your spare time, TJ?' Sir asked him.

There was no response.

'Come on, you must do something. Who do you hang about with?'

'My brother, Jordan, mostly.'

'Didn't know you had a brother,' said Sir.

'He's my stepbrother.'

'Oh. How old is he?'

'Sixteen.'

'Really? So, what do you get up to? What did you do last weekend, for example?'

'We went cow-tipping,' said TJ.

Cow-tipping? What the heck was cow-tipping? Whatever it was, it didn't sound good for the cows.

'What's that?' Sir enquired.

TJ laughed. 'It's pushing cows over. They're not very good at getting back up again.'

Sir was obviously as confused as I was. 'And the cows just let you... tip them over?'

'You have to sort of sneak up on them. And, anyway, they're asleep.'

'Asleep?'

'Yeah,' said TJ. 'Cows sleep standing up.'

'Do they?' Sir seemed puzzled. 'Cows are pretty heavy though, aren't they? Is it really possible to push them over?'

'If there's enough of you, and you all push at the same time.'

Sir pondered this. 'Don't you think it's a bit cruel?'

'Not really,' TJ laughed. 'We chase sheep too.'

I could see Sir's head shaking from side to side. 'And where exactly do you do all this?'

'We go off in my brother's friend's van.'

'And your mum knows all about this?'

No reply.

'You ought to be careful, TJ,' Sir said. 'Somebody said they saw you a few days ago up on the roof of Bettws library.'

My heart went pitter-pat. It wasn't me who'd blabbed.

TJ didn't even bother denying it. 'We was trying out some free-running.'

'What's that?'

'It's where people run and jump along walls and roofs, like stuntmen.'

'Sounds pretty dangerous to me,' said Mr Brock.

'Too right it is. Last week, one of my brother's friends, Hedgy, broke his leg.'

Mr Brock laughed. 'What an exciting and dangerous life you do lead, TJ. School must be pretty boring for you.'

There was a bit of a pause. 'Not really. I like school.'

'Really?' Sir sounded shocked.

There were two complaints about TJ before we even reached main reception. Emily was crying because she said he'd pulled her hair and Ieuan was doubled over, claiming that TJ had kicked him in the 'marbles'. I had never heard them referred to as marbles before.

The first building we came to was a red farmhouse, which was built in 1610 in the Gower. TJ started scraping at the walls with his fingernails. A man wearing a blazer and a badge asked him politely to stop it.

'Why is it so red?' TJ asked.

The man explained that it was to protect the house against evil. An image came into my head of TJ attempting to cross the threshold but being flung violently though the air by the house's protective forces.

Unfortunately, the house let him in. The conditions were cramped, yet he still managed to find room to run around. If he wasn't shouting or running, he was barging into people. I overheard Mr Brock say sarcastically to Miss Harris, 'This is going to be fun – not.'

We didn't learn a lot in the red house. After piling out of it, we made our way through some woods to the Celtic round-house enclosure. As we neared it, I spotted the three hut-like buildings beyond the wooden palisade. One of them was cordoned off with yellow tape as if there had been a murder inside it. We were informed that birds had caused some roof damage.

One of the two remaining houses had smoke belching from its doorway and through a hole in the middle of its roof. There was a class of children already in there having some sort of lesson.

The third house was empty.

Before Sir could stop us, we all poured into it.

We were met by near-perfect blackness. I'm not

fond of the dark. I stood with my back to the wattle and daub walls.

A girl screamed. It sounded like Emily. Hysteria followed. Everyone started screeching and running around as if there was a demon chasing after them. It was pretty obvious who was causing the pandemonium.

One by one, my classmates shot back out of the house.

I remained inside, my back to the wall. I could hear TJ giggling to himself as he trotted towards the door. He must have thought he was the only one left inside.

Sir lost it completely. He yelled at TJ and then yelled at everybody else too, claiming that we were an embarrassment to the school.

A moment later, with perfect timing, a class of children in posh green and grey uniforms filed out of the door of the second roundhouse, in a very orderly and civilized fashion.

'What you looking at, Toffee-nose?' snarled TJ.

Their teacher, who wore a blazer, tut-tutted.

'Sorry,' said Mr Brock, red-faced, leading us inside.

It wasn't quite as dark as the previous roundhouse, but it was majorly fogged up with smoke. We could just about see some logs arranged in a circle for us to sit on, with a fire in the middle. The smoke burned our eyes and clogged up our throats. If I had lived back then, I would rather have lived outside in the cold and wet than in a house like this.

The guide, who was built like a prop forward, started to explain to us about weaving looms, fire-gogs, corn-grinding querns and various utensils, but he couldn't make himself heard above all the coughing. It got worse and worse. Even the grown-ups were coughing.

After a few minutes, Mr Brock surrendered and took us back outside. We poured out through the hole, coughing and spluttering. Some of my classmates fell to their knees. Some pretended to die dramatically.

The guide followed us out, shaking his head in annoyance.

Sir was not having a good day.

We headed for the Museum's centrepiece, a row of six ironworkers' cottages, arranged to represent different periods and create a sort of timeline from 1805 to 1985. There was also a prefabricated bungalow stuck on the end. I remembered from a previous visit that the prefabs had been put up after the war, to create quick homes for people whose homes had been destroyed. They were only built to last ten years but lasted much longer.

Just before we reached the first cottage, we encountered a strange metal construction that looked a bit like a bus shelter.

'What's that?' TJ asked.

'Why don't you read the sign?' said Sir, wiping his brow.

I knew what it was. It was an old-fashioned public

toilet, a urinal made from cast iron. It had been made in Glasgow, but had been used in Llandrindod Wells. Apparently, you used to have to pay one penny to use it. This is where the expression, 'I'm just going to spend a penny' came from. On the little sign next to it, it said. 'Did you know that three years of your life will be spent going to the loo?'

'That's gross,' said Stephanie.

'Come on,' said Sir. 'We haven't got time for that. We're booked in to see the cottages.'

A few children, me for example, were genuinely interested in the history of the houses in St Fagan's. Others were more concerned with getting from one house to the other as quickly as possible.

Not long after entering the cottages, TJ went AWOL. He just disappeared. I could see Mr Brock getting in a bit of a panic, spinning around, pacing back and forth.

I had a good idea where he might be, so headed back past the first cottage. I could hear the sound of liquid against metal. I popped my head around the edge of the urinal.

There he was, taking a pee, in a place you were definitely not supposed to be taking a pee. There was a big sign saying PLEASE DO NOT USE. It couldn't have been any clearer.

He spotted me. 'What you looking at, Four-Eyes?'

I could easily have told on him but decided against it.

'Where've you been?' said an exasperated Mr Brock, bumping into us on the way back.

'Down there,' TJ pointed.

'Doing what?'

'Nothing.'

Sir shook his head and walked away.

*

'When are we eating, sir?' asked Ryan. There was a strong smell of fresh bread from the bakery nearby.

Mr Brock glanced at his watch and then at Miss Harris. It was only 11.45, but we were in a particularly good spot for lunch. There were wooden picnic tables set out, a bit of grass and toilets nearby. The decision was made.

Some of us popped into the bakery to buy some fresh bread and scones. As usual, TJ gobbled down his food in record-time. I saw him secretly drinking a can of LSV. As if he didn't have enough energy as it was.

I overheard TJ ask Sir if he could go and chase some sheep. He'd spotted them as the coach had made its way along the entrance drive.

'Don't be silly,' said Mr Brock. 'You can go and look at those pigs over there, if you like. But don't feed them and don't tease them.'

About twenty metres away was a large fenced-off muddy area, with two sows lying in it.

Mr Jackson took a small group over with him. I tagged along.

'You can see its bum-hole,' said TJ. Unfortunately, you could. The two animals looked asleep. One was on her side, exposing a huge row of teats.

'Do you think they're boy pigs or girl pigs?' Emily asked.

'Are you stupid or what?' said TJ. 'What do those look like?

'TJ,' said Mr Jackson, 'be nice.'

'Is it true that pigs can eat humans?' TJ enquired.

Mr Jackson frowned.

'Only I saw a horror film once, where the bad guys fed this guy to some pigs.'

One of the sows grunted. TJ poked it in the back with a stick he'd just found.

'You're not supposed to touch,' said Owen Jarrett.

TJ glared at him. 'Shut up, know-it-all.'

I was having trouble seeing anything, because the fence was as high as my head. I stepped up onto the bottom slat and leaned over to stroke one of the sow's ears.

TJ gave the fence a sudden jiggle and over I toppled, right into the mud. I started yelling hysterically. I didn't want to be eaten alive. One of the pigs stood up and pushed her snout against me. I tried to run away but my shoes seemed glued to the sticky mud. 'He's going to eat me!!' I panicked.

'It's a she, moron,' said TJ.

'Come over this way, Charlie,' Mr Jackson coaxed, trying to keep me calm.

The pig lay down again. It didn't appear to be interested in eating anybody today.

With a bit of gentle cajoling, I made my way towards the fence and climbed back over, plastered in mud. My shoes brought so much mud with them it looked as if they had trebled in size.

Fortunately, Miss Harris had brought a bag of spare clothes. Completely humiliated, I had to put on an un-ironed yellow t-shirt, and tracksuit bottoms that were too long for me.

'What happened?' said Mr Brock, running over to us.

'He leaned over and fell in,' explained Mr Jackson.

I shook my head in frustration. Mr Jackson was always sticking up for TJ. It was pointless trying to explain what had actually happened.

CHAPTER TEN

ACCUSED

Miss Harris took some of us over to look at the old post office. We squeezed into it like sardines.

'This is smaller than my bedroom,' laughed Ieuan.

'You couldn't even swing a cat in here,' said Ryan.

'Why would you want to swing a cat?' said Emily.

The guide informed us that we were standing inside the smallest free-standing post-office in the whole of Wales.

Just behind the post-office, at the end of a little, curving, downward-sloping path, was a building that looked a bit like the Celtic roundhouses, only it had stone walls, with fairly big gaps in them, like windows, but with no glass. There was a weather vane on the top of it.

'Who lived there?' asked Ieuan.

'Nobody lived there,' explained Miss Harris, 'it was a cockpit.'

'A what?' laughed TJ. He clearly thought that this was the funniest thing ever. He earned himself a major frown.

Ieuan's brow went all sort of corrugated. 'Isn't a cockpit what a pilot sits in, y'know, in an aeroplane?

'This is a different kind of cockpit. It was used for cockfighting.'

TJ was still sniggering away like a lunatic.

'Don't be rude,' said Miss.

'*What??*'

'It was a bit like a boxing ring or a wrestling ring,' she explained, 'only for animals. People would come from all over to watch cockerels fighting each other. It was quite a sport back then. They would place bets on who would win. Apparently, it could get pretty gory.'

'Gory?' said Ieuan.

'There would have been a lot of blood.'

'Cool,' said TJ. 'Can we take a look?'

Miss Harris glanced at her watch. 'If you're quick.'

The boys shot off down the path. I followed. When I reached the opening, some were already coming back out again. I nearly got knocked over as they barged past.

'Boring,' said Ieuan.

'Nothing to see,' said Ryan.

I stepped inside. It was semi-dark. There was a small circular stage or platform, seating accommodation and a promenade.

As my eyes adjusted to the light, I realized that the building now had only two occupants, myself and TJ. We faced each other across the platform, like gunslingers in a showdown.

I spun around and started to walk out. As I did, I

heard hurried footsteps behind me. Suddenly, TJ had wrapped his arms around my neck.

He pulled me down and I felt my face pushed into the ground. I could smell dirt and straw. The pressure on my nose made my eyes water. This was getting to be a familiar position for me. All I could hear was my own laboured breathing.

'What's going on?' said a voice. It was Mr Jackson.

TJ climbed off me. 'Nothing. We were just pretending to be wrestlers, that's all. This is just like an arena.' He helped me up.

I brushed myself down and wiped my sleeve across my eyes.

'Are you okay, Charlie?' asked Miss Harris, appearing behind Mr Jackson.

I nodded, my eyes still watering.

'You'd better keep your mouth shut,' TJ nudged me, as we all made our way to the souvenir shop.

*

For some of my classmates, spending money in the shop was the absolute highlight of the whole trip, in fact of any trip.

The shop was packed with people. There were children from at least two other schools and quite a few pensioners too.

'How much you got?' TJ pestered me, trying to look over my shoulder.

I had three pounds. 'How much have *you* got?'

'I didn't bring any money,' muttered TJ. 'All this stuff is crap anyway.'

He moved on to Owen, who'd bragged earlier that he had a five-pound note. I wondered if TJ was the only one without money. Why didn't his mum give him any?

I picked up some books about castles and browsed through them. Then I found a biro, which had a big blue feather attached to it, like a quill.

Emily and Shannon were looking at some cuddly toys – pigs and sheep and goats and chickens. They had the giggles.

I noticed a security guard watching Ieuan and Ryan closely. They were having a fairly vigorous fight with some plastic swords. He came over and told them to put them down.

Finally, I found something Oliver might like – it was an activity book, with colourings and dot-to-dots. It cost two pounds.

TJ followed me to the counter. 'What are you buying that for, you wuss?'

'It's for my brother.'

TJ shook his head in contempt. He noticed that I still had a pound left. 'Fancy buying me something, then?'

I frowned at him and moved away, but TJ stuck to me like glue.

Thankfully, Sir gave us a two-minute warning and then asked us to line up at the shop door.

'Excuse me a moment,' a security guard called out, striding towards us.

What had TJ done now?

'Yes?' said Mr Brock, looking slightly alarmed.

'I believe one of your pupils has taken something without paying for it.'

Sir looked straight at TJ, who was the picture of innocence.

'Not him,' said the guard. 'Him.' He pointed right at me.

My heart nearly stopped beating. I pulled the activity book from my bag.

'I paid for it,' I protested.

'Not that,' said the guard. 'This.' He reached towards my pocket. Something was sticking out from it. It looked like a feather. It was a blue quill pen, with a label attached to it, saying £2.

'Have you got a receipt, Charlie?' Sir asked.

I was breaking out in a sweat. It felt as if I was on Crimewatch. 'No I haven't. I didn't put it there.'

'Pull the other one,' said the guard, arms folded.

Sir looked confused. He stared from me to TJ and back again. 'But, it's not like him at all,' he said.

'Well, it'll have to be paid for,' he said.

Then the manager walked in, looking pretty irate. He said that we were lucky he didn't call the police and he would make a note of the school's name.

Sir's face was like a boiled beetroot. 'Charlie, I'm really disappointed in you.'

'But...'

It felt as if everyone in the shop was staring at me. My eyes filled up. My distress turned to anger and I flew at TJ, but he pushed me straight back, sending me crashing into a stand full of postcards. They went everywhere, like the playing cards in Alice in Wonderland.

Mr Jackson grabbed hold of TJ and dragged him towards the coach. Sir and Miss Harris helped me up.

Some onlookers tutted. 'What school are *they* from?' I heard someone ask.

'I didn't *do* it,' I yelled.

*

Thankfully, when we got back to school, Sir found about ten pounds worth of souvenir-shop merchandise on TJ and so my name was cleared. There was no way, though, that TJ would be excluded, just for stealing a few things. He'd have to murder someone before Miss Cashman would contemplate chucking him out of the school. She did ring his parents, though.

Owen and I were hovering outside the office when TJ's stepdad arrived. The door was open. We could see TJ slouched on an armchair, his feet resting casually on Miss Cashman's coffee-table.

He spotted me and gave me a fake smile.

Owen waved at him. TJ made a rude gesture back. Miss Cashman shouted, 'Oy.'

With sudden violence, the corridor door was flung

open and a small, stocky man in dirty overalls came striding through. Owen and I moved back against the wall to let him through.

'Where is he?' he snarled.

Miss Cashman popped her head out of her office. 'In here, Mr... um...'

'Bates. I'm his step-dad.'

We both watched in horror as he pushed past Miss Cashman and slapped TJ across the top of the head with such force that he fell off the chair he was lounging on.

'Mr *Bates*!' Miss Cashman called out, holding her hands to her face in horror.

TJ stood up quickly, his cheeks red, his eyes glistening. He looked as if he wanted to kill someone.

'Let's go!' TJ's step-dad roared. 'She's told me what you did, you thieving little git.'

TJ sidled past him, his body tensed, clearly expecting another blow.

Owen and I had our backs pressed right up against a display board.

With unexpected suddenness TJ let out a yell like a wild animal, punched the wall right next to Owen's head, pulled a plant pot onto the floor, kicked a chair, then ran outside.

TJ's step-dad turned to Miss Cashman. 'Don't you worry, luv. I'll sort him out when I get him home.'

'Really,' said Miss Cashman, completely flustered. 'I wish you wouldn't.'

He swaggered after TJ, in no obvious hurry.

Miss Cashman looked as if she'd just been run over by a truck. She spotted us. 'You two, off home now.'

'Did you see that?' said Owen, on the way up the steps. 'I've never seen anything like that in my life, except on the telly. Was that his dad?'

'Step-dad.'

'Holy cow. That was scary stuff.'

CHAPTER ELEVEN

SHOWDOWN AT SHOULDERBLADE

As I mulled over the day's events on the journey back from St Fagan's, the seed for my next story began to germinate.

I wrote at least half of it that evening. Anger and frustration seemed to inspire me. I finished it off on the weekend. This time I word-processed it and printed a copy off.

I gave it to Mr Brock in school on Monday. He said he was blown away by it and read it to the class in installments that week, not revealing who'd written it until he'd finished the whole thing:

CW Underwood's the name and I'm the youngest deputy the town of Shoulderblade, Arizona has ever had. Sheriff Brock says that I have an honest heart and true grit, which is why he appointed me.

I'm not the only deputy. There's also Old Man Jarrett. Gabby Jarrett has an honest heart and true grit too and used to be a sheriff himself one time. Nowadays, he's not so active. He has a serious limp and he's a little too fond of his whisky. Sheriff Brock leaves Gabby in charge of the cells, but he sleeps most of the day.

When my Ma and Pa were gunned down two

years ago, my heart was sore with thoughts of vengeance. For a long time, I wandered from town to town, searching for the killers. But then Sheriff Brock took me under his wing.

Life is good.

The townsfolk sort of respect me, despite my tender age, and, when the sheriff eventually decides to retire, I'm his natural successor. He's taught me how to handle a Colt 45 and a Winchester 73 so that they're almost second nature to me now.

The sheriff ain't the fastest gun in the west but he's surely accurate, resourceful and has nerves of steel. I have seen him disarm men with just a smile and a friendly pat on the shoulder.

I have a hankering to tell you about recent events. It all began with me sauntering into the hardware store and tipping my hat to Laurie Mortensen. 'How you doing Miss Laurie? You're looking awful purty in that new dress.'

Laurie blushed. 'Gee, CW.'

'You sure know how to embarrass the girl, CW,' Laurie's father laughed, putting down his broom and wiping his brow.

I gave a broad grin. 'Hi Mr Mortensen. How's business?'

Laurie had her back to me, pretending to be busy. As I stepped up to the counter, I was about to offer another compliment, but suddenly we all jumped as somebody outside shouted, 'Hey Sheriff!'

The sound of gunfire pierced the air – one, two shots, in quick succession. Spinning around, I checked my holster and made for the door.

The sheriff was on his knees in the middle of the street, clutching his right arm. A young fella lay on the ground near to him. He looked about the same age as me. His hat had fallen off. He was lying completely still.

I took a quick glance around, then scooted over to the sheriff.

He wore a pained look. 'I think I killed him, CW. He jumped me.'

'Who is he?' I said, searching the dead man's pockets.

The sheriff shook his head. 'Didn't really get a chance to see his face.'

'He's young,' I said.

I helped the sheriff to his feet.

He leaned over the body and pulled a face. 'Darn it.'

'You know him?'

He nodded. 'This is not good. That's Jordan Baker. Been making a name for himself lately for all the wrong reasons. He's a cousin of Wild Tom Carter's. Word's gonna get out. We can expect trouble.'

I pondered. 'But I heard Carter had been arrested for a bank robbery. Isn't he locked up in the County Jail?'

The sheriff shook his head. 'Got a telegram this morning. He's escaped.'

Someone had fetched Doc Harris. He bent down, examined the body, then looked up at us, slightly puzzled. 'This man's still alive, Sheriff. The bullet missed his vital organs and went straight through.'

A stretcher was brought over and the injured man taken off the street. Doc told the sheriff that he'd be needing treatment too.

The sheriff sighed. 'When that boy is fixed up, he's going straight in the cells. Carter won't take kindly to that.'

*

A few days later, Jordan Baker found himself lying on one of the bunks in the cells, being talked at by Gabby. The sheriff was sitting in his rocking chair, his arm in a sling.

'I've sent for help, CW,' he said. 'Deputy Jackson from Little Rock will be joining us in a few days – just in case Carter shows up.'

I couldn't hide my disappointment. I took a frustrated kick at the wall.

'Listen, kid, you're about as rough and tough as they get, but I need some experience around here right now.'

I sat down and put my feet up. 'Gee, I've had plenty of experience, Sheriff.'

'CW, you're sixteen years old. I'd rather you be alive to enjoy some more experience.'

'But this Carter fella, he can't be all that bad, surely.'

Truth be told 'though, I had heard that Carter was supposed to be faster on the draw than any man alive. He was as tricky as a rattlesnake, always ensuring he had the sun behind him in a gunfight, so his opponent would be blinded.

'He's a bad 'un, alright,' said Gabby, coming from the cells, shaking his head.

'Have you ever met him?' I asked.

Gabby's brow went all sort of furrowed. 'He's the one who gave me this darned limp,' he muttered angrily.

'Oh.'

The sheriff and I rose to our feet as we heard the sound of thundering hooves from outside.

'Early today,' said the sheriff, checking his pocket watch.

The stagecoach had arrived. Curly-Bob, one of the two riders, had his arm strapped up in a sling. JD Pepper, the other rider, had a hole in his hat. A group of scared passengers alighted. Their jewellery and valuables had been taken from them forcibly by Carter and another man, a Mexican by all accounts.

'That man has a heart of stone,' said one of the female passengers, fanning herself delicately with a pink fan. 'I explained to him that my brooch had sentimental value, but he still took it. And then he had the gall to laugh. I do declare.'

JD handed the sheriff a scrap of paper. 'He asked me to give you this.'

I glanced over the sheriff's shoulder. The handwriting and spelling were pretty dire. It read:

> I'm felling in a gud mood so if you relees my yung cuzzin and put him on his horse and send him owt to Blak Rok by noon tomorro, I won't bother paying your nise littel town a vizit.

The mayor trotted over. He read the note and went deathly pale.

'You gotta release the boy, Sheriff. The town of Shoulderblade is in trouble here.'

Sheriff Brock narrowed his eyes. 'Just hold your horses, Mr Mayor. Just whose side are you on? That kid broke the law. He's staying put.'

'I think you are turning this into a personal matter, Sheriff.'

'Hey, that kid tried to kill an officer of the law, namely me.'

'Exactly, and now you are injured. You cannot ably defend yourself or this town.'

The sheriff stood up. He patted me on the shoulder. 'But I've got my secret weapon here.'

I blushed.

'And he's got me, too,' chipped in Gabby, opening a window behind them. He had a shotgun resting over one arm. 'That darn buzzard won't get one over on me'.

The sheriff walked over and lowered Gabby's shotgun barrel. 'Be careful with that thing, old man, before you shoot someone's foot off.'

A small crowd had gathered.

'You all might as well disperse, peaceable like,' said Sheriff Brock, 'because me and my men here have no intention of releasing Jordan Baker. The town of Shoulderblade holds firm against law-breakers.'

Later that day, the little group of townsfolk returned. In fear of Tom Carter's revenge, they had all signed a petition, demanding the release of the prisoner. But Sheriff Brock was a stone wall.

The Mayor let out a deep, troubled sigh. 'Well, in that case, I'm afraid you can't expect any assistance from us.'

The sheriff's head went back. 'When have I ever asked for help from any-one? A sheriff's job is to uphold the law and to keep his town safe. And that's just what I intend to do, folks.'

Reluctantly, the townsfolk returned to their homes and put their shutters up. In an instant, Shoulderblade became a ghost town.

That night, we took it in turns to patrol the streets. It was about as quiet as a tombstone. The only thing that moved was tumbleweed rolling down the street and the only sound was the occasional neigh of a restless horse.

Just before dawn, the sheriff and I were woken by gunfire and a boisterous yeehaa-ing. We ran to the windows.

Old Gabby was lying in the middle of the street, a rope around his middle. A man dressed in black sat upright on a tall stallion, holding the end of the rope. He had a huge moustache, so big and bushy that you couldn't see his mouth. It was Carter.

The sheriff and I stepped outside.

'Ah, 'mornin' Sheriff,' said Carter, acting all kind of friendly, 'I see you brought your boy with you.'

'I'm not his boy,' I said. 'I'm Deputy Underwood.'

'Well, pardon me, I'm sure,' Carter laughed.

'Let the old man go, Carter' said Sheriff Brock, stepping off the porch.

Quicker than a rattlesnake, Carter drew his Colt 45. 'Stay right where you are.'

I glanced around to see if I could spot the Mexican.

'Last chance, Sheriff,' said Carter. 'All you gotta do is release young Jordan. He ain't such a bad kid. Just a bit boisterous is all.'

'He tried to kill me. He's standing trial.'

Carter frowned. 'Look, Sheriff, let's deal with this in a gentlemanly fashion.'

'I'm all for that, Carter, and you can start by letting Gabby go.'

Gabby wriggled around like a fish on a hook.

'Lively, ain't he?' laughed Carter.

Carter kicked his heels into his stallion's flanks

then started trotting around the street in circles, dragging Gabby along behind him. Gabby couldn't help but let out a few moans as he bounced over the dust and stones.

Sheriff Brock leaned over and whispered in my ear. 'Go back inside, CW, and slip out around the back.'

I did as I was told, making sure my guns were fully loaded. I scooted to the top end of the street as fast as I could. It took just a few moments. Stretching out along the ground, I took a peek at what was going on.

To my horror, Sheriff Brock was now lying on the porch. He looked unconscious, dead even, but I hadn't heard any gunfire. A man wearing a Mexican hat dragged the sheriff's limp body out into the street. Then he scooted into the jail and came out, a few minutes later, with Jordan Baker.

I sat with my back against a barn door, taking deep breaths. What was I supposed to do now?

Staying in the shadows, I found my way to the back of the hardware store and tapped on the door. Laurie let me in. I asked her if I could borrow a bonnet and shawl and her dad's horse and cart. Putting the bonnet and shawl on quickly, I sat up on the cart and headed slowly into the street.

They let me come to within about twenty metres of them.

'We can see it's you there, boy,' Carter laughed.

'Don't be doing nothing foolish. We got what we come for. We'll be heading out shortly.'

'I'm afraid I can't let you go,' I said.

Jordan Baker kicked the unconscious sheriff in the ribs.

'You dirty good-for-nothings,' Gabby said, struggling to his feet.

'Stay down Gabby!' I said.

'Yeah, do as the kid says, old man.'

'I ain't so old that I can't give you a whippin',' said Gabby, as game as a rooster.

Carter gave a tug on the rope and Gabby fell to the ground again, landing on his wrist. I thought I heard something snap.

I went to go for my gun but all three had their weapons drawn and pointed at me before I could even blink.

'You're slightly outnumbered, kid,' said Carter.

Reluctantly, I slid my gun back into its holster. 'You can't just come to our town, and start pushing people around.'

Carter let out a loud laugh. He looked down the street at all the closed doors and windows. 'I think you'll find that I can. Say, how old are you, anyway?'

'Sixteen.'

'Sixteen?' He let out a raucous haw-hawing laugh. 'Short for your age, ain't you? Runt of the litter, were you?'

'I don't have any brothers and sisters.'

Carter nodded. 'Well, you're all alone now, that's for sure. All your neighbours have deserted you in your hour of need. The so-called good citizens of Shoulderblade.'

I climbed down from the rig. I could feel lots of eyes on my back, but no helping hands forthcoming.

'Shall I shoot him, boss?' asked the Mexican.

'Can you dance, kid?' Carter asked me.

'Huh?'

'I said, can you dance?'

With that, he fired off six shots in rapid succession, straight at my feet, the dust flying up around me.

Jordan Baker let out a loud yee-hah.

I stayed as still as a cactus, not because I was feeling especially brave but I could see that these men didn't care whether I lived or died.

'See if I can shoot his hat off,' said Jordan Baker, aiming at the top of my head.

'Let's see if I can blow your head off,' said a female voice right behind him. Laurie stood at the window of the hardware store, an old pistol in her hands.

'Just hold on there, little lady,' said Carter laughing. 'Watch you don't hurt someone with that thing now.'

'She ain't gonna shoot nobody,' said the Mexican.

'No, but I might,' said a male voice. Mr Mortensen had joined Laurie, holding a Winchester 73. Between them, they managed to edge a frustrated Jordan Baker up against the store wall, and truss him up with some old rope.

'Hey, Carter,' I said, 'what say you and me go one-to-one?'

The Mexican smiled. 'Did he just say what I thought he said, boss?'

Carter twiddled a finger in his ear and grinned. 'Naw, don't think I heard him right.'

'You heard right,' I said. 'If I beat you, you leave town.'

He shook his head. 'You won't beat me, kid, and when I beat you, you'll have a hole in your head. You must have a death wish.'

'Hey, you've got nothing to lose,' I persisted. 'You're not afraid, are you?'

The two men guffawed.

'CW, don't be a young fool,' said Gabby. 'He's faster than you.'

'Guess the kid thinks a man's gotta do what a man's gotta do,' said Carter, climbing down off his horse.

My heart was pounding like Apache drums.

'You're not serious, boss, are you?' said the Mexican.

'This won't take long,' said Carter. 'How about we toss this here coin to see which direction we shoot from?'

'I'm happy where I am,' I said, the sun sitting on my shoulder.

Carter nodded. 'You learn fast, kid. Hey, let's do this the old fashioned way.'

'I don't get you.'

'Like a duel. We start back to back, count out ten paces, turn and fire.'

Reluctantly, I took him up on the notion.

There I stood, back to back with the notorious outlaw. I could feel the brim of my stetson pressing into Carter's shoulders.

'Mexican Joe can do the counting,' said Carter.

I had the suspicion that I was being played.

'Uno... dos... tres... cuatro... cinco...'

All I could hear was my spurs rattling and my heart pounding. The sun blazed right into my face.

'... seis... siete... ocho... nueve... diez.'

I spun around.

No sign of Carter. The Mexican casually took some tobacco from his pouch. He giggled. I was sorely tempted to shoot him.

Then, from out of an alley, Carter suddenly dived, rolled and fired. An intense pain shot through my left shoulder. I spun and sank to my knees, my back now to him.

From the corner of my eye, I noticed the sheriff stirring.

Carter stood over my back. 'Not bad, kid, but no cigar. You'd best drop the gun.'

Holding out my arm to one side, I dropped the Colt.

Sheriff Brock was straining to reach out for his Winchester, which lay on the ground about three feet away from him.

I sank back onto my heels slowly, as if resigned to my fate, but I had a second gun inside my shirt, tucked into the front of my belt, the handle pressed against my belly.

'Turn around, kid,' Carter growled. 'I don't much like shooting people in the back.'

'That ain't what I heard,' I hissed.

'Well, you heard wrong, but there's a first time for everything. Unless you turn around, that's where you're gonna get it. I'm gonna count to three.'

There was sudden movement from Laurie's shop window.

'Now!' yelled the sheriff.

I aimed the gun under my armpit and fired three shots, then fell to the ground and rolled over.

Carter's eyes opened wide in horror. Both his hands were clutched to his chest. He frowned, then fell to the ground like a toppled tree.

The Mexican had his gun pointed right at my head.

'Drop it,' said the sheriff. 'Unless you want your head blown off.'

He gave it some thought, but then let his gun fall to the ground and raised his hands.

Concerned for Laurie and her father, I staggered towards the store, but the door opened before I reached it and Laurie ran towards me.

The sheriff, Laurie and I escorted the Mexican and Jordan Baker to the cells where Gabby could have a *nice long chat with them both and make them some bad coffee.*

The mayor burst in. 'There's someone coming.'

The sheriff frowned. He opened the door cautiously. A tall stranger sat before us on a bay mare.

'Can I help you?'

The stranger looked confused. 'I'm Deputy Jackson. Hear you been having some trouble. Thought you might need some help.'

Sheriff Brock looked at me and laughed. 'I got all the help I need right here.'

Laurie planted a big kiss right on my cheek. My face burned red.

'Looks like I missed something,' said the deputy, looking confused.

'You sure did.'

Laurie unhooked herself from me.

I was told later that I came over all kinda funny and passed out.

*

There were quite a few gasps of surprise when Mr Brock revealed who'd written the story.

I'd been watching TJ's reactions as Sir had been reading. He'd definitely enjoyed it. Probably because it had guns in it. He wouldn't accept the fact that I'd written it, though. He shook his head and sneered, 'You copied it from somewhere.'

CHAPTER TWELVE

GUITAR MAN

Last session on Friday afternoons was now Show and Tell in 6B. Mr Brock had seen it on TV in American schools and said that what was good enough for the USA was good enough for Wales.

Seren, Ieuan and Shannon had already had their turn. I was due to go next. My dad persuaded me to take in my electric guitar and amp. He was able to give me a lift to school that morning, which was a good job, because it was all pretty heavy and awkward to carry. I've got two acoustic guitars, one of which I'd started learning on, but the previous Christmas, Mum had bought me a metallic blue Stratocaster.

I put together a Powerpoint and, using this and the Stratocaster, I talked about the different parts of a guitar: the body, the head, the bridge, the tuning pegs, the fret-board, the pick-ups, the output jack, the vibrato arm.

The class seemed genuinely interested. They were also shocked. They had no idea that I could play. I showed them how to tune the guitar and how to use a pick. I explained what the strings were made of and that they were of different thicknesses. I told them what the notes of the open strings were and demonstrated how to use the frets to make the strings shorter.

I soon realized that maybe I was doing a bit too much explaining. Some children were yawning, others were becoming fidgety. TJ leaned back in his chair and fell off, causing a big outburst of laughter.

'Maybe you should play us something, Charlie,' Mr Brock suggested.

'Yeah,' laughed TJ, 'how about Twinkle Twinkle Little Star?'

'Can't play that,' I said.

Sir sat down on a desk. 'Just show us what you can play, Charlie.'

I took a deep breath, then began to play, but immediately made a false start. I stopped playing and readjusted my shoulder strap.

'Not very loud, is it?' mocked TJ.

'Oh,' I said. I'd forgotten something. I stood up and plugged the guitar into the amp.

I played a test note. It was LOUD.

'Whoa!' said most of my classmates.

I played the James Bond 007 theme. The reaction was immediate. Most of the boys held fake-guns in the air. I followed it with the theme from the Pink Panther, which everybody loved and hummed along to. Then I played the intro chord progression from the Black-Eyed Peas' 'I Gotta Feeling'. Within seconds, the whole class was singing along to it.

To finish off, I played some complicated riffs by Metallica. I started to relax and my fingers were loose.

'Wow,' Sir whispered. 'You're a man of many talents, Charlie. How long have you been playing?'

'About five years.'

'Well, that's amazing. Don't you think so, everyone?'

A massive cheer erupted.

'You should go on Britain's got Talent,' said Owen.

TJ had a face like a smacked bum.

'Did you like that, TJ?' Sir asked him.

'It was okay. Pity he can't play Twinkle Twinkle Little Star.'

Sir laughed. 'I expect he could if he practised. Who else in here plays a musical instrument?'

A few hands went up. Recorder, clarinet, violin, trumpet.

'Perhaps we should start our own band,' Sir said.

'Like School of Rock,' said Ieuan.

'Exactly. Well, if anyone wants to practise in here at break-times, feel free, as long as there's an adult nearby.'

I felt as if I was walking on air for the rest of the day. Kids who had never even given me the time of day before now wanted to talk to me. What with the stories and now the music, I felt like a bit of a celebrity.

'Actually,' said Mr Brock later, 'I've still got an old

guitar at home, if anybody wants to start learning. I could bring it in tomorrow. Anybody interested?'

Two arms shot up in the air. One of them belonged to TJ.

Sir nodded. 'Looks like we'll have to toss a coin. Heads or tails, TJ?'

'Tails. Tails for Wales never fails.'

Sir flicked a ten pence piece into the air. It hit the corner of a desk on the way down, rolled along the carpet, wobbled, then landed, heads up.

Owen Jarrett couldn't contain his excitement and started bouncing up and down on his seat. TJ saw an opportunity. He kicked Owen's chair away from him. Owen must have landed on a nerve or something because he reacted as though someone had burned him with a red hot poker. It looked as though he were in agony.

Mr Jackson dragged TJ into the library.

'Didn't want it, anyway!' was his parting yell.

*

I was putting my guitar stuff away at break-time in Mr Brock's cupboard when two people started talking behind the door. I stopped what I was doing and stood perfectly still. It was Mr Brock and Mr Jackson. They obviously had no idea I was there.

'I feel sorry for him,' said Mr Jackson.

'I do too but, you have to admit, he's not easy to deal with.'

'I know, but its no wonder he's like he is. Have you seen the bruises on his arms and legs?

'I assumed he got them fighting.'

'Some of them, maybe. His stepdad actually hit him in the office yesterday.'

'Are you kidding?' said Mr Brock.

'No, I'm not.'

'You saw the way his mum threw him into the room that time. And I've seen other things.'

'How?'

'I live in the next street to him. Do you know what he had for his birthday? Zilch, that's what. Zero. I could have cried when he lost that toss earlier. That kid never gets anything. He'll be in prison before he's twenty. That or dead.'

After a brief pause, Mr Brock said. 'This sounds as if Child Protection Services should get involved.'

'I think they already are,' Mr Jackson said. 'Anyway, better go, I'm supposed to be on duty.'

The cupboard door opened and Mr Brock's eyes opened wide. He went bright red. 'Charlie? I had no idea you were in here.'

I tried to walk past him.

'You heard, didn't you?'

I nodded.

'I'm sorry,' he frowned. 'You weren't supposed to.'

I frowned. 'Do you really feel sorry for TJ?' I asked.

Mr Brock smiled. 'You and TJ don't exactly get on, do you?'

'He hates my guts.'

'D'you know, I don't think he does. He just needs someone to take his frustration out on.'

'I heard what Mr Jackson said about the guitar,' I said. 'I've got an old one that I don't use any more. Maybe TJ could have that.'

Mr Brock looked blown away. 'That's really, really kind of you, Charlie, considering how he's been towards you.'

'Well I can't exactly fight him back, can I? He's a lot bigger than me. Maybe this is a better strategy.'

Mr Brock smiled. 'It's definitely worth a try. Don't hold out too much hope, though. TJ has a lot of barriers to break down. I'm not sure how he'll respond to kindness. I don't think he's used to it. It's got to be worth a shot though. Anyway, go and get some fresh air.'

He stopped me at the door and told me he was proud of me.

*

I decided that I couldn't wait until Monday. The following day, a Saturday, after my usual trip to the library with Oliver, I told my mum that I was going to call for Ieuan, but sneaked out the back door with the guitar and headed in the opposite direction. I was taking a massive risk. I felt like one of the heroes in my stories.

I knew where TJ lived – right at the back of the estate in the roughest part – but had never been there. It felt more as if I was heading for a dragon's lair than a classmate's house and I nearly turned back a few times.

There was a rusty car in his garden. I couldn't work out how it had got there. There was no driveway or garage but somehow the car sat on the lawn, behind a little white fence. The tyres were all flat.

I took a deep breath, opened the gate, walked along the short path and tapped on the door.

Some shouting erupted from inside, then TJ's mum answered the door, fag in hand. 'Yeah?'

'Uh, is TJ in?' I asked. I never thought I would ever say those words.

She frowned, then turned around and yelled so loud that the windows rattled. 'TJ, get down 'ere!!'

'What?!'

'Don't *what* me! Get down 'ere!'

There was no response.

She pulled a face. 'Come on in a minute, luv.'

I followed her inside. There was a baby crawling around on the floor. His nappy must have been full because there was a strong waft of poo, mixed in with the smell of damp and wet dog.

I noticed that one piece of wallpaper was hanging half-off. There was some graffiti over the fireplace. It had swear-words in it. A camp-bed lay in one corner of the living room, with some of TJ's stuff lying on top of it.

I spun around as he walked into the room.

He looked like he'd been hit by a truck. 'What the hell do you want?'

My heart beat rapidly. 'I was wondering if you wanted this guitar.'

'What?'

'What's wrong, TJ?' said his mum.

'He wants me to buy his guitar.'

She looked at me. 'Can't afford it, luv. How much?'

'Nothing.'

She laughed. 'You're kidding. That's very nice of you. It's a waste of a guitar, though. He'll probably smash it by the end of the week.'

TJ threw himself down on the sofa and switched the TV on.

His mum stared at me as though I were an exotic fish. 'So, you're one of TJ's friends. Didn't know he had any friends. How's he doing in school?'

TJ glared at me.

I gulped. 'Okay. He's good at sport and making things.'

She looked confused. 'Well, well, what a shocker. He's actually good at something.' She lit another fag, scooped the baby up under one arm and disappeared into the kitchen.

TJ stared at the TV screen. He was watching a horror movie. 'Don't come to my house again.'

I rested the guitar on an armchair. 'You can have it. Really. I don't need it.'

'What?'

'The guitar. You can have it.'

I left it on the chair and headed towards the door.

'Are you serious?'

'Yeah.'

He looked totally confused. 'How am I supposed to learn how to play it?'

'I could teach you a few chords to get you started.'

He still had the remote control in his left hand. Reaching over with his right, he grabbed the guitar. 'I suppose I'll have it, then.'

Not a thank you or even a smile.

He started strumming on it. It hadn't been tuned and sounded awful.

'Anyway,' I said. 'It's yours'

I opened the front door and walked out, accompanied by some pretty discordant guitar sounds.

I let out a huge sigh. It felt as if I had been holding onto my breath in there. Maybe, just maybe, I thought, that by this gesture, I had succeeded in making my life more bearable. All my fingers were crossed.

When I got back to the house, Mum wanted to know what I'd done with the guitar. She'd spotted me leaving the house with it. When, with reluctance, I admitted to her what I'd done, she shook her head in utter disbelief. 'Are you crazy? Are we talking about the boy who beat you up?'

'He didn't beat me up.'

'He made your nose bleed. Are you off your head?'

'I know what I'm doing'.

I wasn't so sure, though.

*

Over the next few weeks, TJ definitely eased up on me a little bit. There were a few snide remarks here and there but nothing I couldn't handle.

One weekend, I was sorting through my guitar books and found a beginner's book that I no longer needed, so decided to take it over to TJ's. Ieuan came with me.

As we climbed off our bikes and rested them up against TJ's fence, we heard an almighty row coming from inside the house.

'Let's go,' said Ieuan. 'Now is obviously not a good time.'

A downstairs window suddenly swung open and something came flying through the gap, landing with a twang on the lawn – if you could call it a lawn. It was more like a rainforest with a car in it.

We stood on tiptoes to see what the UFO was. It was the guitar, thankfully still in one piece.

From inside, I heard TJ let out a shriek. He sounded like a wild animal. The door opened and he came running out of it. He picked up the guitar and examined it all over. Luckily, the long grass had cushioned its fall.

A small shed sat in the corner of the 'lawn'. TJ

marched over to it, went inside and emerged with a metal toolbox. It looked very, very heavy.

'Don't you dare!' a man's voice called from the still open window.

TJ opened the box and tipped it upside down, spilling the contents all over the grass.

His step-dad stormed out through the door, grabbed TJ's hair and started pulling his head back and forth, while calling him all the names under the sun.

We dropped to the ground, behind the car.

'Did you see that?' Ieuan whispered.

'Gerroff me!' yelled TJ.

Mr Bates growled 'You can put those tools back in the box right now and you better make sure everything is in its proper place.'

TJ stood up, kicked at the scattered tools and went to walk back inside the house.

His step-dad pushed him to the ground 'Do as you're told!'

'Mum!' yelled TJ.

'It's no good calling her. Either you pick them up or I'll smash the guitar.'

He tried to grab it but TJ held on fast.

TJ's step-brother Jordan stood at an upstairs window, laughing like a hyena.

The dad called up. 'Oy, Jord, come and give us a hand.'

Jordan pulled his head in and, a few seconds

later, ran out into the garden, wearing just a pair of jeans.

Between the two of them, they managed to pull the guitar from TJ and push him to the ground.

'Smash it,' said the step-dad.

Jordan smiled a malevolent smile. He lifted it above his head as if it were a sledgehammer.

'Don't,' pleaded TJ. He started to put the tools back in the box, muttering to himself. He wasn't crying, though. After a few moments, he closed the box and put it back in the shed. 'Now give me the guitar,' he said.

'Say please,' said the step-dad.

'Please.'

'Say pretty please,' added Jordan.

'Get lost.'

With that, Jordan lobbed the guitar into the air. It bounced off the car and landed with a thwump on the grass.

TJ ran over, picked it up, examined it carefully, growled, then headed for the door. His step-dad and brother both clipped him across the head as he walked past them.

The door slammed shut.

We sat with our backs to the next door neighbour's wall.

Ieuan shook his head. 'Uh, I don't think it's such a good idea to give him that book right now.'

'I could leave it at the door,' I said.

'Are you kidding? You're taking your life into your hands.'

I offered Ieuan a chewing-gum. 'He's got a pretty awful life, hasn't he?

Ieuan shook his head. 'Doesn't look like a lot of fun.'

I rolled the book up, quickly stood up, ran to the door, shoved it through the letter-box, then spun around quickly, only to collide with Ieuan who, unbeknown to me, had followed me. We sprawled to the ground in a tangled mess.

'What are you doing?' I hissed.

'Following you.'

'Aaaarrghh!' cried a voice from inside the house. 'I'll kill you!'

We heard some thuds and the sound of something breaking.

Then, to our horror, the back of TJ's head banged against the window and stayed there, rigid. There were hands around his neck.

'Let him go, Dad,' Jordan's voice pleaded. 'He's had enough.'

TJ's face appeared to be going blue.

I got to my feet, banged on the door really loudly, yelled 'Police!!' and ran for it.

Ieuan and I clambered onto our bikes and started pedalling like crazy, just as the back door opened.

I heard a woman's voice shout after us, 'Bloody kids.'

I couldn't believe what we'd just witnessed. It was like one of the families off the Jeremy Kyle show.

CHAPTER THIRTEEN

JOY-RIDE

If what had happened wasn't awful enough, something a lot worse happened a few days later. Something that none of us could have expected.

Our class had spent the morning at the high school, meeting some of the teachers we'd be having next year. It was nearly lunchtime. We were about to head back to school but, as I had a dentist's appointment that afternoon, I had to catch a bus home.

TJ was going home for lunch too. He told Sir he was going to wait for his step-brother, Jordan, who was due out of class any minute.

Sir pondered this for a moment.

'Here he is,' pointed TJ.

Mr Brock relaxed, glanced at his watch and then led the rest of the class off.

I was about halfway to the main road when I realized I'd taken a wrong turn. An impossibly tall fence blocked my path, meaning I had to head back the way I'd come. The bus was due any moment. I started jogging.

Taking me completely by surprise, somebody stepped out from in between two parked cars and nearly knocked me off his feet.

It was TJ. 'What's up?' he said.

I tried to edge past him. 'I need to catch the 12.20,' I said, out of breath.

'We'll give you a lift, then,' said a voice from behind TJ. It was Jordan. He stood next to the open door of a silver people-carrier. It clearly wasn't his vehicle.

I tried to move past TJ, only to be confronted by Jordan's friends, two big lumps called Wayne Fogarty and Dean Higgs.

'Let's go for a ride,' insisted Jordan.

Wayne and Dean grabbed my arms and start pulling me towards the open door.

'Don't be daft,' said TJ, looking concerned. 'You can't just kidnap him.'

'Who's asking you?' said Jordan, slapping him across the head. 'Thought you didn't like him, anyway?'

TJ was ordered to climb in. He didn't look happy. I was bundled in after him. Dean, the slightly larger of the two lumps, blocked me in. Jordan took a quick glance around, then climbed up into the driver's seat. Wayne perched beside him.

'Welcome aboard,' said Jordan, grinning. He reached forward and started the engine. Someone had left their keys in the ignition.

As Jordan reversed out of the parking space, a pair of fire-doors in the school building flew open with a loud clang and Mr Waring the PE teacher came bursting through them, dressed in a black tracksuit.

'My car! My car!' he virtually shrieked and started sprinting towards us.

'Where are we going, Jord?' Wayne enquired.

'Dunno yet,' said Jordan, seemingly unconcerned. 'Barry Island? Bristol Zoo? Oakwood?'

'You're gonna need more petrol, then,' said TJ.

Jordan glanced at the petrol gauge. 'Crud!'

Dean swivelled around, bumping me on the shoulder. 'He's gaining on us!'

Mr Waring looked as if he was going to explode.

Before us, at regular intervals, lay a series of speed bumps. The maximum speed in the school grounds is 10mph.

Jordan hit the accelerator and we headed flat out for the first bump. 'Yee-hah!!' he whooped.

Mr Waring stopped running and cradled his head in his hands. Jordan's manoeuvres weren't exactly doing his car's suspension any good.

I held on tight for the second bump but it didn't make any difference. The result was exactly the same. We were like eggs in a basket.

'Faster!' shouted Dean.

'Hold on to your kegs,' Jordan laughed as we hit the third bump, flying through the air and landing with such a jolt that we nearly skidded off the road. It was like being on a bucking bronco.

Jordan ignored the Stop sign at the end of the school lane and went to pull straight out into the main road, but had to come to a screeching halt as a kid came running out of nowhere, right across our path.

Unbelievably, Mr Waring drew level with us and started pounding his fist on the door, nearly caving it in. 'Oy!' he called out as we set off again, rollicking over the top of a mini-roundabout, right across the path of an oncoming blue Fiesta.

'Watch out!' yelled TJ.

Jordan scowled. 'Who's driving this thing, me or you?'

'You are, but I don't feel like dying today.'

He shook his head. 'What's the nerd's name?'

'Charlie Underwood.'

Swivelling around, he said. 'My brother doesn't like you.'

I stared out of the window, resigned to my fate.

TJ folded his arms and scowled. 'You do know you're gonna be expelled for this, Jord.'

There was no reply.

We travelled a couple of hundred yards, then headed into an Esso garage the wrong way, narrowly avoiding a head-on collision with a motor-bike.

Wayne jumped out and quickly put in about twenty pounds worth of petrol. One of the cashiers pointed at us through the window, then headed out towards us. Wayne slammed the nozzle back in its holder and jumped in while the people-carrier was already moving. The cashier had to virtually dive out of our way as we exited.

We shot back out onto the road and Jordan started swerving the car from side to side like a lunatic.

'Where are we going?' TJ asked.

I felt a bit sick. My head throbbed. I could see Jordan grinning in the mirror.

'I thought we'd pay a little visit to our old school.'

Jordan, Wayne and Dean had all gone to Our Lady's. They'd left four or five years ago and the head-teacher back then, Mr Griffiths, had been more than glad to see the back of them, from what I'd heard.

We made a sharp right turn off Monnow Way into Parret Road and then squeezed through the school gates, smashing a wing mirror off in the process.

Year Three were on the yard playing benchball.

'Oy oy, there's Mrs. Bowen,' Wayne pointed, then added, 'She didn't like me.'

'I wonder why not,' smirked Dean, 'You're so loveable!'

The people-carrier paused, revving up like a bull waiting to charge.

'You can't be serious, Jordan?' TJ said.

'They can run, can't they?' Jordan sniggered. He pressed his hand on the horn for about ten seconds and then made a rude gesture towards his old teacher.

'Quick,' I heard Mrs. Bowen say, 'get out of the way everybody! Over here! Over here!' She shepherded the children towards a grass bank.

One kid obviously wasn't listening, Riley Price, blonde with a Mohican haircut.

Mrs. Bowen screamed 'Riley!' as we crept up behind him. As he turned around, he found himself nose-to-nose with a car as big as a tank. All the colour drained from his cheeks.

Jordan started revving the engine really loud.

Riley backed away slowly. His mouth looked as if it was trying to form words, but his brain obviously wasn't working properly.

Jordan revved even louder. Riley tripped over his own foot and fell to the ground.

'Did you see that?' laughed Wayne, hysterically.

I saw my chance and tried to get out but Dean spotted my move and hooked me back in. Jordan shoved the car into gear and we continued forward.

Mrs Bowen appeared out of nowhere and started pounding on the side of the door. 'You absolute IDIOTS!' she yelled. 'What do you think you're doing?'

Jordan leaned across Wayne and shouted through the open window, 'Get lost, you old bag!'

'YOU!' she yelled, recognizing him.

'Yeah, it's me,' he yelled back, giving a silly little wave. 'D'you want my autograph?'

'STOPPPPP!!!'

The voice belonged to TJ.

Jordan slammed on the brakes and the car came to a halt.

'What? WHAT!'

'LOOK!' gasped Dean, pointing ahead.

'Where'd he go?' Wayne said.

Dean pointed downwards.

Mrs. Bowen put her hand over her mouth. 'Oh!'

I shot past Dean and pulled the sliding door open. He put his foot out as I tried to get out, causing me to topple to the ground, landing with a shoulder-wrenching thud.

I spotted Riley, lying between the two front wheels, thankfully not *under* them. Picking myself up, I helped him to his feet and led him around to Mrs Bowen.

'Charlie?' she frowned. 'What's going on?'

'I think he's alright, Miss,' I reassured her. 'He must have tripped. It looks like the wheels missed him.'

'Idiots,' she said. 'All of you.'

'But...' I started to say as Dean pulled me back inside.

Jordan turned around, grinning. 'Right. Let's go and cause havoc somewhere else.' He threw the car into reverse.

'Look,' said Wayne, panic on his face.

'What?' said Jordan, glancing towards the school building.

'It's Jonesy.'

It was indeed Mr Jones, who must have witnessed the recent events from his workshop window. He looked like a man on a mission. He wouldn't bother with small-talk. A few weeks ago, a local teenager wandered onto the yard at lunchtime, up to no good. Mr Jones literally carried him off the yard to the office and phoned the police. Someone said he still had the kid under his arm while he was on the phone.

Jordan put the people-carrier into a big, reversing arc, screeched to a stop facing the gates, then put into first gear and pushed his foot down.

Mr Jones was running straight towards us. It looked as if he had no intention of getting out of the way. Was he honestly thinking of playing chicken with a people-carrier?

'Holy cow!' Wayne bellowed, his hands covering his eyes.

'Keep going!' urged Dean. 'He'll get out of the way!'

'Why don't *you* drive?' yelled Jordan. He stayed on course. There was going to be an awful mess in a matter of seconds.

At the last moment, we swerved slightly as Mr Jones clattered into the side of the Previa and bounced off it. The vehicle actually wobbled before it scraped and clattered through the open gates.

TJ kicked the seat in front of him. 'You could have killed someone, you moron!'

Jordan turned around and thumped his leg. 'Shut up. And watch who you're calling a moron.'

As we headed back out onto Monnow Way, I heard the blare of a siren. Bettws police-station was in the shopping centre just up the road. Jordan turned left and headed back towards the high school.

A crowd had gathered at the mini-roundabout that we'd driven over ten minutes previously. Mr Waring stood there, along with a large group of curious bystanders, clearly beside himself with rage. Like Mr Jones, he was another person not to be messed with. Apparently, he did mixed martial arts in his spare time and had once sparred with Joe Calzaghe.

It was he who saw us first and actually tried to run in front of us, but Jordan swerved left, travelling half on, half off the pavement and nearly colliding with a lamp-post. We headed towards Malpas Road, the main road that leads to Newport and the M4.

'Crap,' said Jordan, slowing down.

Flashing blue lights headed towards us. Re-enforcements! The oncoming police-car veered across the road, blocking our way.

With one police-car behind us and one in front of us, we had no choice but to drive back into the High School.

'What do we do now?' asked a worried Wayne. All exits would be blocked in a few seconds.

'Shortcut,' declared Jordan, seemingly not at all bothered. He jumped the people-carrier over a kerb and onto the sports field, which was full of teenagers enjoying their lunch-break. Without hesitation, he headed out across the grass. He didn't seem to know where he was going because he meandered all over the place, sending kids sprawling left and right. There were quite a few screams and near-misses. An overweight kid, in a panic to get out of the way, tripped over his own feet, sailed through the air and landed with a thud.

'Look,' said Jordan, 'an acrobatic hippo!'

'Nice one, Jord!' Dean guffawed.

'Yeah,' Jordan grinned, 'how many points do I get for that one?'

'Where's this shortcut then?' TJ piped up.

Jordan's head weaved from side to side. 'There's a gap in the fence along here somewhere.' He slowed down a bit to try and get his bearings.

'Get out of my car! Right NOW!' a voice yelled.

'Aaaarggh!!' cried Wayne. 'It's Waring!'

Jordan threw the car into reverse and we sped backwards with Mr Waring hanging on to the side. We just managed to avoid slamming into the rugby posts, but not without scraping the side of the car and snapping off the remaining wing-mirror.

Mr Waring fell to his knees. It looked as if he was having some sort of breakdown.

A police car pulled up next to the people-carrier and two officers flew out of it. Jordan waited until they'd got right up close, then sped off again, searching for his so-called gap.

A second police car arrived on the field and headed straight towards us. We were being forced towards a huge ditch that ran alongside one edge of the field. Jordan accelerated.

'What you doing?' Wayne gasped, a note of panic in his voice.

'We're gonna jump this ditch. If I pick up enough speed...'

'Don't be mad, Jord!' said TJ.

Jordan spun around in his seat and glared at him. He looked as if he'd lost the plot completely.

I gripped my seat with both hands. I remember thinking *We're not gonna make it.*

The police car behind us slowed right down as if to give us a chance to reconsider, but Jordan was in no mood to back down.

The field of spectators stood there, open-mouthed, as the Previa built up speed, reaching thirty, forty, fifty miles per hour.

This was not good. I made doubly sure my seat-belt was fastened.

'You're gonna get us all killed!' TJ yelled.

This was starting to feel like we were in some sort of action film, like 'Speed', where Keanu Reaves jumps a bus over a huge gap in a flyover. Only this wasn't make-believe and no special effects could help us.

The ditch rushed towards us.

There was no turning back.

No time to brake.

'Here goes!' yelled Jordan. 'Hang on to your Y-fronts!'

The people-carrier left the ground.

It was as if we were travelling in slow motion.

I put my hands in front of my face.

Please God, please God!

SOUTH WALES ARGUS

Saturday June 22nd

DEATH RIDE

Sadly, a juvenile prank went terribly wrong yesterday, leading to one teenager being killed and four being badly injured. Jordan Bates, aged 16, was killed when the Toyota Previa he was driving crashed into a ditch in the grounds of Bettws High School. Dean Higgs and Wayne Fogarty, also aged 16, and Thomas Carver and Charlie Underwood, both aged 11, were passengers in the vehicle and also received injuries which were later reported as being non-critical. The older boys had stolen the Previa, which belonged to Mr Anthony Waring, a Physical Education teacher at the school.

After driving around the estate and into a local primary school, the boys took the vehicle onto the sports field of Bettws High where the driver lost control.

Of Jordan Bates, the head-teacher, Mr Clement, said, 'He was a troubled lad. My heart goes out to his family.' A police spokesman commented, 'Sadly, this event demonstrates the dangers inherent in any criminal behaviour.'

CHAPTER FOURTEEN

NEW CHAPTER

A week later, I was back in school, still a bit shaken by the whole experience. No bones broken though, thankfully.

The week after that, TJ returned. While he'd been off, Miss Cashman had held a special assembly for him and his family. It looked as if he had lost some weight. And he hardly spoke.

At lunchtime on that first day back, Owen and I agreed to help Mr Brock with the Book Fair. Twice a year, three big metal trolleys were delivered to the school, full of books, posters and stationery for sale. Sir needed help taking the money and recording what had been spent.

We opened up the trolleys. The shelves were brimming with new books, the latest by Dave Pilkey, Michael Morpurgo and Jacqueline Wilson. There was also a box with posters in it of football teams, maps, puppies, kittens, celebrities and bands. And another box full of pens, pencils, rubbers, sharpeners, key rings and bookmarks.

The hall was swarming with kids, most of them without any money, just browsing.

TJ was hovering around. From what I could see,

it looked as if he was deliberately taking books and putting them back on the wrong trolleys.

Mr Brock went had a quiet word with him, but he still lingered.

Before Sir could stop him, Owen went over to him and said, 'Do you intend to buy anything?'

TJ held up something. 'I'll be having this later.' It was a James Bond spy kit in the shape of a small briefcase. I knew it cost £9.99. I'd already sold one of them. 'My mum's gonna bring me the money after school,' he said. 'What time do you shut?'

The Book Fair was open from 3.30 to 4.00 as well as at lunchtimes.

A few minutes later, he brought a book over to us. It was a long, narrow book called Guitar Chords. 'How much is this?' he asked.

'It says on the back,' said Owen, leaning over my shoulder.

'No it doesn't.'

Owen took it from him and pointed to the bottom corner. The price was on there, though admittedly very small. 'That'll be five pounds,' he said.

TJ looked at him as if he was from Planet Zog. He turned away and, true to form, went and put the book back on the wrong shelf on the wrong trolley.

He turned his attention to the posters, ruffling through them and managing to rip the corner of one of them, taking off some of Justin Bieber's head.

'Sir,' Owen gasped and pointed.

'Don't worry about it, Owen,' said Mr Brock.

*

TJ came to the Book Fair every day that week, lunchtimes and after school, but never actually bought anything. His mum was supposed to be coming, but she never did.

At 3.55 on Friday, TJ was still there, hanging about.

Mr Brock went over to him. 'Sorry TJ, but we're gonna have to close up.'

'Whatever,' TJ mumbled. 'I hate books anyway.' He reached forward, pulled a few books onto the floor, then ran out the building, leaving Sir looking visibly upset.

As we'd helped out all week, Sir said that Owen and I could have a free book each from the trolleys, up to the value of £5. I found the book I wanted and headed out to the bus stop, just as a bus pulled off.

TJ was sitting on the kerb. He spotted me. 'Looks like you missed your bus,' he laughed. Another one would be along in ten minutes.

I avoided standing too near to him. He looked as if he wasn't in a good mood. Thankfully, he ignored me.

I glanced through the pages of the book I'd bought. I recognized most of the chords and quickly memorized some unfamiliar ones.

I had an idea. Taking a deep breath, I edged closer to TJ. I held the book out towards him.

TJ scowled at me. 'What?'

'I thought you might like it.'

TJ stared at it as if it was a piece of gone-off food. 'Get lost,' he said, snatching it from my hands and throwing it into the road. A lorry drove over it.

'What the heck!' I yelled. My bottom lip started to quiver.

The passing traffic splashed TJ's legs. Soaked and dirty, he refused to move.

A few minutes earlier than expected, the next bus arrived. I jumped on and went upstairs to my favourite spot at the back.

As the bus turned a corner, I watched as TJ got to his feet, scooted out into the road and retrieved the book. He dried it off and put it inside his jacket.

I smiled a satisfied smile.

*

TJ and I never mentioned the book again, but on the following Monday, TJ brought my old guitar to school. He asked if he could stay in at break-times to practise with me and Ryan. Mr Brock thought it would be a great idea. I tuned it for him.

Mr Jackson sat at the computer while we practised. At first TJ did his own thing, jarring discordantly over the top of what Ryan and I were trying to achieve.

Then he asked us to show him how to play an A minor chord.

He was a pretty quick learner and absorbed everything that Ryan and I taught him.

Over the next few days, he made such quick progress that he could soon play simple chords along with us. His sense of rhythm had miraculously improved since the disastrous music lesson that had ended with me throwing the wooden block and being sent to the office.

The three of us learned a piece together, each of us playing different parts. It wasn't bad at all.

With a guitar in his hand, TJ became almost a different person. He started treating me like an actual person, not like some small creature from another planet.

'Did you really write that story about the cowboys?' he asked me one day, during one of our practice sessions.

I nodded. 'Why, did you like it?'

He shrugged. 'It was okay, I guess. Pretty funny. How do you do it? Make up stories, I mean.'

I pondered. 'I read a lot. That helps. It gives me ideas.'

'I could never do anything like that,' said TJ. 'I'm thick.'

'No you're not,' I said. 'You're good at things that I'm not good at.'

'Like what.'

'Making things. Sport. Swimming.'

TJ actually smiled. 'Maybe you could you put me in one of your stories,' he said.

How could I tell him that he'd already been in most

of them already? After all, it was he who'd been the inspiration behind the Whomper Whoomper Snicker Snacker, Karvrog, Blackheart and Tom Carter.'

'What's so funny?' said TJ.

'Nothing. I could write a play. Me, you, Ryan and Ieuan could perform it in our Leavers' Assembly in two weeks time. Also we could play some guitar music at the beginning, that piece that we've been practising.'

TJ looked concerned. 'What would the play be about?'

'Dunno yet. I'll have to have a think about it.'

That evening, at home, I started writing the script. It was about a young monster who feels like the odd one out in his family of monsters. He is the white sheep in his family of black sheep. He decides to venture out into the big, wide world. Along the way, he meets various characters and learns how not to be a monster.

*

The last day of Summer Term – and my last day in primary school – came around frighteningly quickly.

The Leavers' Assembly was a great success, although Mr Brock had a bit of a wrist-slapping from Miss Cashman because it ended up being two hours long. Sir was keen for us to show off *all* our talents. During rehearsals, the assembly grew longer and longer as more of us stepped up to the mark. In its final version, it resembled Britain's Got Talent, with gymnastics, acting, poetry, trumpet playing, karate, even origami.

TJ, Ryan and I received rapturous applause for our guitar piece and for the short play we performed.

Mr Brock bought all of us a packet of felt pens each and he wrote cards for each of us, with personal messages inscribed on them.

With five minutes to the end of our last day in primary school, we had a bit of a sing-song. Then Mr Brock shook hands with us, one-by-one, as we filed out. Some of my classmates even hugged him.

*

But that wasn't the last I saw of Mr Brock that day.

Just as my bus was pulling off, Sir came bounding up the stairs, briefcase in hand. He looked pretty tired. Teaching must be an exhausting job.

'Well, well,' said Sir, taking the seat in front of me, 'Charlie Underwood. I thought I'd seen the last of you.'

I smiled.

'Looking forward to the high school?'

'Sort of.'

'What's not to look forward to? New teachers, great facilities and resources, new friends. I just know you'll do very well. You have so much talent.'

I was a bit apprehensive about the big move but that's perfectly normal, isn't it?

'You and TJ seem to be getting on a bit better these days.'

'I know,' I said. 'I didn't see that one coming.'

'Neither did I. You've done so well. In fact, to use football parlance, I think you've played a blinder. It's funny how music can pull people together, and stories of course. I liked your play, by the way. Very insightful. Maybe, you should be a psychologist when you grow up. That's of course if you're not having books published or playing in a band.'

'Thanks. Are you staying on at Our Lady's, Sir?'

'Oh yes. A bit of good news. I was only on a temporary contract but Miss Cashman wants to make me permanent. And I thought she didn't even like me.'

'People are hard to read sometimes,' I said.

'A truer word was never spoken.'

Mr Brock glanced out of the window, then stood up. 'My stop, I believe.' He tapped my forearm. 'Good luck, buddy. Keep in touch. Let me know how you're getting on. And TJ of course. I'll be the first in line to buy your books or watch you in concert.'

He reached the top of the steps and turned around. 'Now, don't forget, the world is your lobster.'

That didn't sound quite right.

I watched Mr Brock break out into a jog along the pavement.

The bus pulled off, leaving behind an old chapter in my life and taking me towards a new one.